A Centimeter Across the Earth

A novel by Samuel M.

A CENTIMETER ACROSS THE EARTH

First edition. March 1, 2024.

Copyright © 2024 Samuel M..

ISBN: 979-8224791446

Written by Samuel M..

For all the outsiders, wherever you are. Wherever you may be.

<u>**Prologue:**</u>

There is fire in a land of endless rain.

It always rains. No matter the time, no matter the weather, no matter the circumstances. It's been so long, I find it difficult to recall if there was ever a moment in which I didn't feel the rain. It always follows. No matter where I am, no matter what I do. The entirety of the land which surrounds me is always downcast and colorless. Endlessly dripping, sopping.

When the fire came, it refused to leave. Even with the rain battering down upon it, still it burned on. Brightly, defiantly. But there's more to it than meets the eye. More so than that, I think the rain fuels the fire somehow. They've made a pact, you see? In exchange for teaching gloom and indifference-methods on how to be disconsolate, the fire gifts to the rain death and destruction. Demonstrating the lesson that all things will end. Ideally in a violent, ever-consuming rage. The rain never stops and the fire always burns. They've become codependent on one another, this fire and this rain. At this point I find it hard to believe that one can truly exist without the other. I am always reminded of that, no matter which path in this land I choose to travel.

The rain has followed me my whole life. The fire is what reminds me I am right.

This fire does not represent warmth. This water does not represent life. And if I make it out of this place alive, I worry that these truths will remain unchanged. It's a twisted irony, having discovered this, because change is one of the things I fear the most in this life. Maybe I've already grown accustomed to them. Maybe I won't want them to change at all. What if the thing I really want is this fire and this rain to grant me some sense of finality-and with their help, refuse to play the game I have become ensnared in. The horror is, whether it be in this life or in all the other lives that come after, a game must always be played-and this game is always the same.

What's really strange to me is that I've never actually learned how to play the game. I could be playing an entirely different game than everyone else as far as I know. There is, simply put, no way to tell. Has the role I've taken on forced me into playing the game differently? Is it the trail I have chosen that's amplified this? Was it this particular choice in fact, that is the root cause of my difference in methods? Whichever way it's spun, it doesn't matter. Deep down, I know that to not play it outright is what I truly desire.

The mere discovery of this thought is enough to make me shudder.

I've been fighting in this war for so long that the moment in which I felt the fire entering this land has become hazy to me. Of course, I can pinpoint the exact instance in time, it's just the feeling of it that eludes me. After having witnessed so much atrocity, I now perceive the horrors of this war as simply a daily routine of monotonous drivel. Each and every day I wake up, greeted with the stench of rotting flesh. Whenever I emerge from my tent, the only thing I manage to see are limp human bodies being carried on stretcher after stretcher after stretcher. At the end of every day those bodies are the only thing I can recall about it. No other thoughts except the thoughts of bodies. They're in the food I eat, the ground I walk, the air I breathe.

There have been instances in which my own flesh and bone have sustained damage, but injuries have never mattered much to me. I usually make it a point to brush them off. I have always been one to place my mental and emotional turmoils far above my physical ones. I hold them to much greater importance. Physical injuries are just inconveniences, some greater than others sure, but nothing more than that.

I have learned to become numb and unfeeling during my time as a soldier, although "learned" is a generous term. My time as a soldier is more akin to the practice of striking an unsuspecting child into obedience. I always take my orders as they come. I act and I act and I act, but never do I ask. I know well enough not to do that, and it always pleases my superiors. It ensures that I am left alone. Nothing else to be asked of me, only ever protocol. Despite my time as an actor in the grandest of all performances, the stage to end all stages, this war has changed nothing at all. That fact makes me wonder sometimes about the implications of the fight I am in. I've tried to gain a deeper understanding of it. I am entirely unable.

From time to time I think back on my life before this war. Do what most people would call "reminiscing," but I have great difficulty recounting fond memories whenever I take the time to reflect. They appear in my head tainted for some reason. I experienced what the average person would consider a normal life before I joined the war, but I feel no different now as I did back then. What has all this dreadful experience done in service to me? The only reason I joined the war effort was because I'd been caught in a moment of weakness. A moment of unfiltered fear and uncertainty and desperation. At the time I believed being in an army had, at the very least, certainty. It had an outcome. It wouldn't leave me lost to fumble around in the dark. When the recruiter came to persuade me, he managed to offer some sense of security-and to be honest it felt reassuring, being part of something much bigger than myself. How naive I was, but now that I think back on it I wonder what I would've done had I refused that offer. What direction would I have chosen to go? Where would I have ended up? If I'm to be truthful with myself, if given the option, I would've liked to hide somewhere far, far away. Hide there until the end of time.

The life I led before the war was one of triviality. Completely inconsequential. I don't, can't recall any moments of excitement or intrigue. Even if there were, they have all but slipped from my memory. If it's that easy for me to forget them, they probably weren't worth remembering anyway. There were no true struggles I had to endure. No lessons that ever stuck with me. I was given everything I could ever want or need. And yet... I felt so empty. After taking in all considerations I am sure that something went missing. A crucial part of my genetic makeup that should have been there from birth failed to materialize. A fundamental aspect to being. There are fractures in the base of what I am.

I've noticed that there's this barrier between me and other people. Something inexplicable that keeps me from understanding them. I've had moments of success from time to time, but that's all they ever are. Brief moments. That impenetrable wall always appears in some form or another. Whether it juts up out of the ground suddenly or falls down from the sky gradually, I end up separated from the other party. The only consistency I can give to myself is this same inevitable result. I've come to understand that all relationships are tenuous, insubstantial, fleeting. I can't ever truly know another in this life that is so quick and to the point. Composed of brief sparks that leave as quickly as they came. That's what I've come to take away while in this war. Seeing all this life be snatched away in an instant serves as a constant reminder. That's all there is to it. If one's life can be taken so easily, then it stands to reason that the parts that make up one's life can as well. Though oddly enough, the people I'm surrounded by tend to have more difficulty in taking the latter.

Each and every one of my attempts at living has resulted in failure. I can scavenge around for quick flashes of relief. Doing so in order to keep this reality at bay, but what will I do once there's nothing left to scavenge? I seriously doubt that I am compatible with what surrounds me at any given moment, even my own parents I find hard to understand. I can't seem to comprehend who they are. It shakes me to the core, how very little I know of the ones who brought me into this world to begin with. There are also friends. Before I left my friends and I had plenty of laughs and occasional moments of tenderness. I'd like to think back on all whom I have met fondly. Still I worry that what I have with them will slowly start floating away. It probably has already. How good can a memory be if it leaves you bitter and full of regret?

But in spite of all of this, I can't help but hope for something better. To wait for a day when I can finally belong. For despite everything else, hopefulness still resides stubborn and headstrong within me. Hope truly is a twisted invention. Maybe the most twisted human invention of all. It always manages to well up inside me no matter the state I am in. It's like an abusive household that hurts you over and over again; but no matter how many times you come back, it always welcomes you into its home with open arms-and once again I find myself standing at hope's doorstep. Fist raised, ready to knock on that door.

I told my parents and my friends, everyone I know really, that I was leaving to fight and that I would be discharged precisely 920 days from the moment I left. Everyone told me that they'd be ready when the day came. If not then, they reassured me it would definitely be someday.

I hope they wait for me.

Will you wait for me?

Act One

1.

My tour is finally over.

When the news reached our combat site that night an expansive relief washed over me. As the news spread I could hear the occasional yelp of excitement coming from this way and that. I carried myself with an air of exuberance for a good while after. And it wasn't just me, this was the aura that traveled throughout every inch of the grounds that night. Our elation couldn't be contained and in a lightning fast domino effect, a full celebration broke out. As I walked around the site observing my fellow soldiers, I couldn't resist sharing in all their excitement and happiness. What was in the air felt absolutely contagious. All of them possessed such brilliant, jubilant spirits. Spirits that soared higher than any I have ever seen. They were all getting along with such ease. As I looked on, something dark suddenly stirred within me.

Luckily, there was plenty of alcohol going around.

I've always found alcohol to be an effective tool for dulling the senses, for dulling the mind. I'm not too fond of myself when I'm sober. No one else really is either. There have been many nights in which I've drunken myself to sleep while sitting stuck inside my tent. My troop gets all the drinks we want without, strangely enough, any issues. Each time I'm alone with a bottle I sink promptly into a delightful insensitivity. Falling away from everything around me and most importantly, myself. I really do find it a much better way to spend the nights. Besides, I'm willing to bet that many of my fellow soldiers do the same. There's plenty of pain to go around in this place, a truly oppressive amount. Everybody has something they're trying to numb.

Now most of the time I try my absolute best to stay at arm's length from the rest of my outfit. I have no desire to be a part of whatever sort of clique they've constructed, and I'm sure that feeling is mutual. However tonight is a special occasion. I won't ever see these people again once I return. So I figure I might as well join in, even if for only a moment. But there's no way I could just waltz into their company like I've been there from the start. Intrude by latching onto them like some parasite. I resolved then to find another way in. To become undetectable, to remain at all times on the outskirts of their celebration. Yes, I will simply observe them. Watch what makes them tick. See what they are able to do so easily that I somehow can't. But before all this is set into motion, I need to drink.

As I stumble my way towards this site of celebration, I keep thinking, "What kind of tragic comedy is this?" Just yesterday we were cutting our losses and bearing an insurmountable weight of dread upon our shoulders. Today we are dancing like jesters for a silent king, not a care in the world. Our ability to adapt is astounding.

As I turn the corner, I witness a fight break out. I can't quite discern what the argument is about. Their voices are completely unintelligible. Flying forth in a sloppy, drunken haze. I thought maybe to put a stop to it, but it quickly fizzled out into nothing more than a petty squabble. Even quicker, the two made up and departed the scene together as if nothing had happened. No matter how many times I witness it, I am still left in awe. Our adaptation skills truly are remarkable. No other species can change at the drop of a hat like that.

Lurching back towards the celebration now. I've almost arrived. I can feel the presence of some outside force latching onto the side of my brain, beckoning me into it. It tempts me, comforts me, it's washing all my worries away. The party roars back into view. I witness people moving, dancing, laughing, conversing, drinking. And in the center of it all lies a pit of fire. It's mouth frothing. It's tongue licking the air. Held back only by the binds the soldiers have put on it. Maliciously destroying everything that has the misfortune of being tossed into its jaws. The binds look as if they are about to break at any moment. There is fire, so much fire. The only thing that surrounds it is darkness.

I sit just on the edge of this great gathering. I wait. I watch. I listen. The information I'm trying to absorb, still it's beyond me. I can't grasp any of it at all. I find it such a struggle to understand. I'm going to leave this place having learned nothing aren't I? I'm beginning to see that there was no point to this excursion. I should've known that before even making the attempt. I should've known any attempts were to be futile. I think it would be better if I were to disappear. I think that would be good.

But as I got up and prepared to leave, I was stopped by the presence of a drunken, bumbling old fool. Immediately I recognized him, he was one of the most beloved combatants in our squadron. So well known that without ever seeing his face you could have guessed who he was. He had what you could consider quite the status among the rest of the troops. He was surprisingly adept at combat and was even awarded multiple badges of honor for his contributions, most of which he was wearing when I ran into him.

That doesn't make him any less of a fool. I fear not those who can only destroy the body.

I don't really remember his name. I never asked. In fact I don't think I've learned a single person's name in all the time I've been here. It's all just one massive blur that I've been eagerly waiting to leave behind. Thinking about it now, it dawns on me that this is the first conversation I'll have had with someone while being on this tour. Not a passing nod or a communication of reconnescience or a meaningless congratulations from one of my superiors. An actual, genuine conversation. No one else here has granted me one, and for that reason alone, I will cherish what little time I have with this fool no matter what.

As I regained my bearings and prepared myself to face him, he just as quickly threw his arm around me, laughing with a thunder that effortlessly echoed across the campsite. Almost as if everything had suddenly paused so that the laughter could make its way. He took a fast yet somehow prolonged swig from his handle of liquor and grinned, "Such a Lovely night tonight. The air is still and gives no warning signs. No bastards coming to ruin our victory eh?" he laughed. I wasn't sure what victory he was referring to. From what I've gathered we haven't been able to conquer much.

I replied "No sir."

The soldier and his badges of honor looked a bit surprised, but there was a glint of satisfaction in his eyes that was unmistakable "Sir huh? Oh I like you already. What's your name?" he asked.

I did not give him an answer. In that revealing moment I decided to refuse. There was an indescribable unpleasantness which radiated from this fool out of every pore. I realized now how mistaken I was in even entertaining this interaction. Once again I had acted out of desperation, and once again I am paying the price. If my heart can be swayed this easily, what other traps will my frail frame fall for?

"Not much of a talker? Don't worry about it. That's alright with me." the soldier with his badges of honor said "I can see by that look on your face that you already know who I am. You've at least heard of me no doubt." He took another drink and put on a calculating expression as he finished "My heart is so full tonight. You know why? It's because all these beautiful soldiers, these beautiful people-who came here to dedicate themselves to their nation, are going home. Who can finally be at ease for the first time in over two years. Even if it's just for a little bit. Whether they know it or not, they've all earned their seats in Valhalla. The sacrifices they've made to make their nation proud have been well regarded by those who live above. This celebration is well deserved."

It took everything within me not to laugh in his face. What a truly pitiable fool he was! He had deluded himself with these ridiculous fantasies of heroism, making it abundantly clear that he genuinely believed in every word. It became apparent to me that he was a man who placed all of his value on those tiny little trinkets he had strapped to his chest. There was nothing else to him. No dreams or feelings or ambitions about anything else. But what really baffled me the most, was that he seemed entirely content with this. If given the choice, I am certain he would rather spend the rest of his life fighting in this war than going home. Maybe that was the problem. Maybe it was because there was no home for him to return to...

The old fool sighed longingly, then turned to me and said "Well, I'll see you around. Maybe when we get back to base." And just like that our conversation, more accurately our lack thereof, was over.

Amazingly enough the exchange left me emptier than I was before. I couldn't wrap my mind around what had just happened. It felt as if I merely blinked and the fool with his spangled army jacket had left. All I could do was feel my chest beginning to grow itself a hole, one I am quite familiar with. Every interaction I have with another person ends up becoming the cavity through which this hole begins to form. Always feeling by their end confused and aloof. Growing on and ever stranger the more time I spend with one. Why is it that I find every human being so incomprehensible? I end up discovering less and less a proper solution to this question the more of them I engage with. Surely there is an answer out there somewhere, waiting to be found. I refuse to believe that there is no answer. I have to find out. I must know why it is this way.

Before I knew it, this conviction I was seized by had me searching for the first person I could find. The person who could save me from this predicament.

I circled my way around the fire, looking feverishly for a sign.

Three laps around and I still can't find what I'm looking for. Every which way I look, there are people of all sorts permeating in droves. It should be easy, but I can't simply choose any ordinary person. No, I need something else first. An indication from someone that there is more to them than meets the eye. I'll know it when I see it. I'll know them when I see them, I'm sure of it. My eyes darted everywhere, head on a swivel.

That's when I saw her.

From across the way, nestled in between all the activity and simultaneously distant from it, she sat. Hands resting silently beneath her. She presented herself in complete stillness, gazing out at something far removed from here. Despite all the hustle and bustle of the crowd she had no problem standing out to me. Her eyes had an intense hardness to them that drew me in without hesitation. They were so dark that the only thing I could make out were two swirling black beads floating in a sea of chalky white. She was deep in thought, contemplating what I could only begin to dream of. What it was appeared impossible to decipher. I knew then and there that she could help to answer my question.

Walking the distance to meet her now, this soldier with her beady black eyes is forever burned into my memory. I sensed that the instant my eyes found her. I feel a burst of my own excitement, something I haven't felt in quite a long time. A rush so sudden and intense that to my surprise my feet still are left unswept. I know exactly what I'd like to ask. I'm not here to meet her necessarily, but rather for the knowledge and expertise she could provide. I know she possesses those gifts, and in that moment it felt like I too was about to get my hands on the resources she held so well refined.

As I make my way over, she spots me. For the entirety of the time it takes to reach her, our eyes never part from one another. At that moment, we immediately understood each other. We both found what we were looking for. No introductions or pleasantries or small talk will be getting in our way. Everything that should or could be said upon first meeting a person doesn't need to be. It never did to begin with. Only what's been building like bile in our throats, aching for a way out, will escape from our mouths tonight.

I sat down perpendicular to the soldier with the dark empty eyes, looked her dead in the face, and without further hesitation asked, "Do you know what the opposite of sonder is?"

She looked a bit taken aback, almost uneasy, but recovered instantly, "What exactly do you mean?" she replied, her tone suggesting she entirely anticipated something like this.

"I mean that in all the words to exist or to ever have existed, across every lexicon, there is not a single one that accurately represents an antonym for sonder. So what is its opposite?"

The soldier with the beady black eyes sat in silence for an infinitely long moment, taking in what I had just said. After this eternity passed she responded, "The word you're looking for is solipsism."

I shook my head "But that doesn't quite cover it. That term and its definition could never cover it. Other minds cannot be truly known, yes, but solipsism entails a belief that those minds do not exist in any capacity. That outside of your perspective lies a barren wasteland with nothing to discover. How then would you make your way about the world? Does this line of thinking not breed ignorance? Am I expected to believe that your mind doesn't exist, that you don't exist?" I sat, staring her down, eagerly awaiting a response. I felt my right hand beginning to shake ever so slightly.

Looking up with her twin pair of voids, the soldier replied "Depends on your perspective I suppose. I've always had a strong distaste for what people consider to be 'real.' The definitions for existence and those designations which are so commonplace fill me with disdain. That's your problem too. Since you're at least partially opposed to this idea, this may be where our similarities end."

It was my turn to be confused, "I don't understand, why now do our similarities end?"

"Because you're trying to come to terms with some objective reality." she said. "Looking for a problem to solve where there is none. I see it in your face. You are so desperate for a solution to your dilemma that you felt the need to come to me. I am almost certain you can find the answer on your own."

I sat in silence for an uncomfortable amount of time, completely stunned. My head tried wrapping around, seeing if there was something about her I could figure out. I came up empty. This is least of all what I expected.

"You believe only your mind is real, don't you?"

The soldier with the beady black eyes shrugged, "It's easier this way, I've found. Detachment from what humans call reality has made me all the more content in remaining with my own. What is inside my mind, my heart, my body, my nerves, that is my reality. In here there's no need to compare myself. No need in trying to measure up. No reason to reach out for others in a desperate, futile attempt at connection. I simply remain outside of it all, instead huddled comfortably in my own microcosm. You want that too, don't you? Isn't that why you came to me?"

Her gaze then became so intense that I had to avert my eyes.

I shook my head, "No, that isn't why. What I'm searching for is connection. To have just one person know me inside and out is all I ask. To hold with another a bond so tight that even Excalibur couldn't sever it. In hindsight I expected too much. I understand now how different we are."

She threw back her head, howling with laughter, "For a person with such loaded questions, the way in which you approach your dilemma is painfully simple. Do you think that's all there is to it? That once you know everything possible there is to know about a person, your job is finished? Say you were able to achieve this, that you discover every aspect of someone and there's nothing left to find. You alone know them the best. That means nothing. The morning after they'll be different. Something in their mind will have changed, possibly everything. Who knows, their very foundations may well have shifted. Once you cross that finish line, the moment you lay your head down to rest another thirty or one hundred or four hundred meters will be waiting for you when you wake up. And you won't have a clue as to how it got there. It'll be far too late by the time you realize that you have entered into an endless race. The same person is never the same person twice. Not at any moment in time."

This gave me pause. Is that what it was? Is my problem purely unsolvable? If that is the case, her methodology might not be a bad idea. Maybe I do want to selfishly remove myself from the concerns of the world. Maybe I did just despise human beings all along. I've been excommunicated from a sense of belonging for as long as I've lived, what difference would it make if I started now?

Unfortunately for her, and for me, I refuse this offer. I had almost forgotten whose doorstep I'd been waiting on.

I chuckled a bit, "All this sounds tempting, I'll admit. You've given me plenty of things to chew on."

I stopped to inhale before beginning again, "There is a part of me that believes in your message. It would make this hell that we call existence much easier. But that's not the solution I'm looking for. I've had that desire many times before. That wish to be closed off from the world because you're ensnared in fear and mistrust. I'm right there with you, I'm still stuck in that place."

The soldier looked at me with her beady black eyes, "So what is the opposite of sonder?" she asked.

"I don't think there's a word for it really. The bitter truth is that at the end of the day, we are all utterly alone in this."

"So why reject my solution?"

"Because I am certain there is something other human beings have that I don't. A missing link that, if latched on, will allow me to be a person properly. Even if I can never know anyone, I'll at least be able to live amongst them. Once I learn what that one thing is, only then will I experience sonder. Only then will I be connected to the human race." I said.

"Are you sure that's all it will take?"

"I know that's all it will take. That has to be all it will take. Because I don't know what to do if it doesn't." my voice trembled.

The soldier with her beady black eyes sighed and stood up, "Well good luck to you. I never found any answers in all my time spent searching. I don't think an answer exists to be honest, but I hope you find what you're looking for. I really do."

We looked at each other one last time in a moment of pure understanding. Born separate from my own preconceived notions. Our spirits weren't quite kindred but I felt then and there at ease. Our eyes lingered.

She turned heel and disappeared into the night.

The fire suddenly felt colder.

2.

At some point in the night I'd managed to find the way back to my tent somehow. When I awoke this morning I was laid spread eagled across my thin, wilting mattress pad. Nothing else really happened last night, but my memory is hazy. Either because I was too drunk or because I chose to place a cloud over it. Regardless, tomorrow is the day I get back to base. The day after I am going home.

As I sat on the edge of my mattress trying to collect myself, I heard a rustle from outside my tent followed by a muffled voice, "Is anyone in there?"

I slowly peeled back the tent flap, wondering what the matter was this early in the morning.

One of our combat nurses was standing there. Blood which dried like paint was splattered across their uniform, "The lieutenant wants to see you, he's waiting in the war room."

The war room was what all of us referred to the higher ups tent as. It's easily the largest tent on this site, with plenty of room to spare. It's also where all the strategies and deliberations for killing take place. I've caught bits and pieces of the discussions they've had. They're similar to a group of friends debating on where to eat. There's also plenty of laughter.

As I walk towards this tent, I wonder what the lieutenant could possibly want with me. Hadn't he just arrived the other day? Surely there are other matters far more pressing that need to be tended to. With each step brings more unease.

When at last I entered, I was immediately met with the smell of cigarettes. A tray with ash that was dying and soon to be snuffed out sat at the edge of the enormous tabletop. As my eyes traveled to the end of it, the table soon gave way to the torso of a man who I was supposed to respect. He stood with both his fists pressed against the table. The last of the cigarette still clenched between his knuckles.

The lieutenant smiled, "Hello Private."

"Hello lieutenant." I responded. I never speak unless spoken to.

"Do you know why I summoned you here today?" he asked

"No sir, to be honest I don't have a clue." I replied matter of factly.

"Now that is surprising. You seem to have no recollection of your own merit." his face was beaming.

What is this? What is he getting at? I suddenly felt warmth in my chest, a warmth that I believed to be foreign to me. Was this the first time I'd experience kindness in over two years? I was so desperate for it that even a man such as him would suffice.

"I'm sorry sir, I don't understand what you mean." I managed to blurt out.

"Be proud today, private. I've been informed by your superiors of the heroic deeds you committed during this tour. You saved a total of ten lives, isn't that correct?" he ventured.

"Yes sir, that is correct sir" I said.

So that's why I'm here. It's all rushing back to me now. I accomplished the task of making sure people weren't killed. Something that I believed to be basic human decency turned out to hold some kind of tangible, measurable value. The warmth in my chest quickly retracted itself.

"Now that is something to be proud of isn't it? Putting your own life on the line for the sake of others. Diving headfirst into combat not only to harm, but to help. That's a very, very brave thing to do, private." he grinned.

"Thank you sir." I said.

The lieutenant reached into a box about the size of the ashtray it was sitting next to. He pulled from it a small, rounded piece of metal. It shined bright and bronze from the light peeking in through the tent. Attached was a piece of cloth with a pin threaded through its fabric.

"I'd like to award you with this. In commemoration of your services. It's a badge of honor. Honor in every sense of the word. Honor to its utmost degree. Be aware of what you have accomplished, and wear it with pride." he uttered this with conviction.

"Thank you sir." I said, taking the piece of metal from his outstretched hand.

"Go now and wear it for all to see. Depart with the knowledge that you are a hero private." he declared.

So I did as he said, and left the lieutenant without a word. My head was spinning. I felt a sickness residing in my stomach.

I need some distance from all of this. Just for a little while. I have the time now. I want to see what's around me. I haven't seen or looked at anything really. In all the days I've toured this place my surroundings still remain foreign. I'd like to take it all in before I leave. See what I saved those people from. See what it is we've been fighting for.

I walked through the camp, past the final row of tents, and arrived just on the outskirts of the nearby forest. I made my way through all of its messiness and all of its density. For a moment becoming completely lost in it. I never did come across a path. I then found myself on the forest's other edge, looking out into a clearing. There was nothing in that clearing except a dried up dead looking basin formed by some man made horror or another. The only thing I could make out was the color grey. Grey on the ground and grey in the air. I looked up. Ash was drifting slowly, gently, quietly, through the sky. Everything was still.

So this is the result of two and a half years of war.

Before I knew it I was laughing to myself. It feels almost liberating. Almost as if this war's meaninglessness had adverse effects on its mongers. Like they are now suffering the consequences for every expenditure. The demons who waged this war have gotten nothing out of it. Thinking about this simple fact made me very pleased. All that fighting to gain nothing. I have no sympathy for them. They are all cowards who flee the moment they see the whites of my eyes. I can only wish for their punishment to well fit their crimes. I have my doubts, however, if any punishment shall ever arise.

It's astonishing what little this war has done for me. The lieutenant talked at length about my "honorable" deeds, but his praise is a hollow shell that echoes out to an age that has long since passed. I am certain that he believes to be in combat itself a source of honor. Quite frankly, it's something a child would think. But at least children have the capacity to grow.

In all the time I've been here, I never killed. I plainly refused. When out on the battlefield, I did everything in my power to stave off that outcome. Witnessing all the life around me become cut short in the blink of an eye did that. So many people with so much complexity and history to them ended with such ease. The speed at which these soldiers' lives end, the instantaneous nature of death on the battlefield, makes me break out into a cold, pale sweat. Such blatant disregard for human life is what spurred me to protect what I could of it. I resolved especially to prevent myself from experiencing this outcome. If I am to die, it will be on my own terms. The idea that I would be, and am, viewed as nothing more than a sack of flesh for these demons to play with fills me with contempt. So call my deeds heroic if you'd like, there's nothing about this that's courageous.

There's such a disconnect between all of us here who are fighting. All this tension and resentment. I've seen it rear its ugly head plenty of times before. Every soldier here keeps the other at arm's length. Because I think that above all, we're afraid of each other. Terrified of the hell that dwells inside of us. Each and every one. A lingering sense of dread permeates throughout our squadron. It's there at all times. Even if one of us manages to establish a bond with another, the tears begin showing themselves shortly thereafter. There's nothing heroic about this. This grotesque thing that we call war. To think it could accomplish anything has to be one of the greatest lies ever told. The whole time I've remained here, I've done nothing but float and drift wherever the war machine takes me. I have existed as a living corpse for the past two and a half years, but I think that's a good thing. Maybe that's just what I needed.

A reset button, a chance to do it all over. Maybe some good will have come from this. Maybe now my life can finally begin.

Starting tomorrow, I hope I can rejoin the human race. I must be able to.

This war has changed nothing for me, although nothing I did before going off to fight was of any consequence. I never really did things. Rather it was things that happened to me. I seem to lack the capacity for agency. The few times I did possess it ended rather poorly for me. So I learned to keep my head down and my mouth shut, reflexively pushing away any sense of autonomy I presented myself with. No matter how much the urge tried to claw its way out, I knew I would be no match for the eyes which gazed upon me as a result. A pair of eyes is one of the most horrifying things in the world. Whenever I look into them they reflect back onto me an entity so freakish and abhorrent that the eyes discover just how incompatible they are with it.

I had the opportunity to change. I had reached a point in my life that was chalk full of transition. Full of endless budding branches that I could have tended to, nourished. Instead I chose a fly trap that tempted me with sweet talk of insurance and guarantees. By the time I woke up, I was shrouded in a claustrophobic darkness. Such a stupid, stupid thing for me to do. All this life has ever been is a constant struggle. My body and my soul have been put out to slaughter more times than I can count. Is that what the fruit of all my efforts have come to? Are these the benefits of my fight? Most people say the struggle is what builds you up. They say it's actually what makes you stronger. Gives you a fighting chance against the world. Helps you grow into the best version of yourself. All of this I've found to be a demonstrable lie. Emerging out the other end of all this pain and strife, I feel nothing but bitterness and loathing and hatred. My struggle does not make me strong. All it has taught me is that the world is composed of indifference and omitted empathy. As some kind of remedy I've been reassured countless times that everyone else struggles in these ways, as if that's supposed to be a comfort. As if all the suffering in the world somehow doesn't make this place worse. This earth is full of useless pain. That's the lesson I've learned.

It dawns on me that I haven't achieved anything. I have failed at living. I've fallen behind and I keep falling behind every moment I stay here. I wonder what I could have achieved had I chosen something, anything else. There's still so much work to be done. The position I've been in my whole life needs fixing. This war has actively delayed that process. There are skills a person gains by being on this earth. Experiences that every human being has at least once in their lifetime. I have been sealed off from them. Denied the chance to even try. I was forced to take up arms, invariably leaving behind the things a human's life should be. The more I think about this, the more livid I become.

If a God really does exist, he's going to have to beg for my forgiveness.

All I can see is red. The more I think about these things, the more venom I struggle to choke back. I can feel rage boiling my insides. It fills up my entire body. Someone must be punished. Someone must answer for the hell I've gone through. There is not a single chance I will allow these crimes to roam free from consequence. Somebody has to pay, but who? Everyone in this camp is in the same position as me. They've already been punished plenty enough. I can't think of anyone that would suffice.

The lieutenant.

The moment it dawned on me, I knew it was to be him. Of course it was him, it had to be. He stands for all the anguish and strife I've been subject to these past few years. He is a representative of the demons that sit high upon thrones made out of human bone, playing with their fleshy pawns however they see fit. The lieutenant is one of the commanding officers after all. He commands how each day's suffering is going to go. I will not let him get away with it. I must stop him. I now know what needs to be done.

I'm running quickly back to the campsite now, fueled entirely by a single purpose. I am a soldier after all. It is my sovereign duty to see my missions through to the very end. The sun is setting now. The last few rays of its light soon to be snuffed out. Night will soon be falling all around me. It will give me the cloak I need, and I will wait. The air will be completely unmoving. The universe will watch in silence.

I stood over the lieutenant's bed. Silently, I watched him sleep. He was not restless nor was he tense in his slumber. He was perfectly happy and content. The most comfortable person I'd ever seen. Nothing of any importance weighed on his conscience. He was free from any guilt or shame. All he did was lie there in pure, unfettered bliss, not a care in the world.

I smothered him to death that night. I hid the pillow among the other belongings in my tent.

3.

The next morning they found his body. No evidence of violence or any indication of a struggle. Those who found his body said it was a tragic, freak accident. Somehow he had died in his sleep. An event that was completely unpredictable. Everyone in the camp was brought to a brief funeral service for the lieutenant. It was too expensive to transport, deliver and maintain the body, according to a message we'd received back at base. I'm too bothered to find out why money was the most pressing issue.

It was decided that our service to the lieutenant would be a funeral pyre. We cremated him in the same spot we held our celebration. Some other officers in rank said a few words to commemorate and say goodbye to our beloved lieutenant. What those words were I couldn't say. I'm sure they were very touching. The fire was lit, and it burned. It burned the lieutenant so brightly, so hot. Its jaws swallowed him whole until all that remained was ash, then dust, then emptiness.

The fire almost burned all the rain away.

And just like that, it was time to leave. Nothing else needed to be done. Time marches ever onward.

The army trucks had arrived, packed and ready to take us to the train station.

But before we left, I asked if I could run back to see if I forgot anything.

"Sure thing, just be back soon. Train leaves in ten minutes" one of the officers said.

I made sure that I was out of sight before turning and heading towards the pyre. When I arrived, I saw only a few logs remaining in the aftermath. They were coated in embers that burned faintly, almost extinguished. I circled the pit over and over again, constantly swinging my head back and forth for signs of danger. I gazed one final time at those last few logs, almost caught in a trance. Something is pulling me towards it...

I had to make sure the lieutenant was dead, I needed the reassurance. The consequence of that pyre convinced me well enough.

Quickly snapping out of it, I gathered myself and turned around back towards the trucks.

After all this time, I'm finally going to see everyone again. Riding on this train back towards the base to meet them and I'm just now realizing it. This is the first time in eons I've allowed myself to look forward to something. I have stood at the doorstep of hope for so long and now I'm finally reaching to ring its doorbell. It feels genuinely surreal. I'm almost dizzy thinking about it, like I have the sense that a revelation is coming soon. Maybe it really was just being entrenched in war that made me so vile. If that is the case, being a person shouldn't be too hard at all.

I wonder how much has changed since I've been gone. I hope not too much. Change is something I'm extremely averse to. If things have changed too much, or the difference between myself and others is too noticeable, I'll surely be left behind. Thinking about this keeps compounding my worry. A thought like a seed that's been planted in my mind, growing wilder and more out of control with every minute that passes. Change is a cold, callous creature. It doesn't wait for anyone. It never has and it never will. It attacks with silence, inflicting upon its victims melancholy and regret which endlessly spread-leaving as quickly as it comes. Thinking about what this creature might do to me has made my past miserable, more so than I ever should have allowed. Although my fears aren't entirely unwarranted.

The opposite of love isn't hate, it's indifference.

Having to endure indifference places more strain on me than I could possibly bear. A terror far greater than I could comprehend lies in that outcome. I must be able to avoid it at all costs, but what other alternative might there be to that fate? I'll have to think of something.

That may be the key to moving forward. If only I can figure out what that alternative is.

As I sit riding the train back to base, I can't help but think about these things. Mountains pass in the blink of an eye, carving and imposing their shapes onto the wide open skyline. A skyline dull and uniform. Every tree we pass is dead. Flowers and shrubbery bend to the train's will as we roll along the tracks, clinging desperately to their roots. All of this soon gives way to a wide rolling field. Oceans of grass yellow and withered make ripples in the crust of the earth as a hard wind blows. The further along we travel this grass sprouts less and less until all that's left is cold, dead earth. This cold, dead earth is soon replaced by piles of rubble and an ocean of bones with no more flesh attached to them. I realize as I look around that we now pass through a town very clearly the victim of scorched earth raids and carpet bombings. This must have happened during our tour. I heard no word about it spread. No news at my camp broke out. Looking around the rest of my car, no one else seems to mind too much the carnage laid out before them. Out of the corner of my eye, I notice two grunts in uniform laughing and snickering to each other.

My head was pounding, right then I felt incredibly nauseous.

All of this sums up perfectly why I've kept myself secluded. Why I refused to learn any names. Why I know nothing about anything or anyone. These people are worse than animals. There is nothing any human being could have done to justify the outcome of that raid. Ghastly doesn't even begin to cover it. Yet everyone around me seemed to act like nothing was wrong or were actively celebrating. They have no fear, just instincts. None of them were taught survival or companionship or honor, just cruelty. And they learned to master that cruelty a long time ago. They've long since perfected it, maximized it, leaving little room for anything else in their hearts and minds. One could argue this is the ideal method to raise a soldier. If you think about it rationally, it is the most effective way at winning a war. The soldiers on this train had no choice. No one here was taught any better.

It doesn't matter. I hate them. I hate them all.

Below my feet the train's wheels began making an odd creaking sound. It started slow and subtle at first, but soon the sound crescendoed and enveloped the entire train. We slowly grinded to a halt, stopping at an overpass looking out onto a river that snaked its way into the horizon. There was silence then followed by murmurs of confusion. A few minutes later the car door slid open, presenting in its doorway the conductor.

"Sorry everyone, looks like there's been an engine malfunction. We should be up and running momentarily."

Many groans and complaints ensued.

The conductor raised his hand, waiting for the noise to die down. Then at last he said, "Don't worry, we'll still be arriving at the base as scheduled. Thank you for your patience."

The conductor's announcement did little to comfort me. Even if we do arrive on time, the fact still remains that we are making no progress. I desire to end my book's chapter as a soldier as quickly as possible. How many more obstacles must I face before it's finally over? The more time that passed, the more restless I grew.

"Jesus, this sure is tedious isn't it?" traveled a voice from behind my seat.

I turned my head to look behind me. Sitting there was a man with a face that was radiant and full of light. He looked young, around the same age as me in fact. He had dirty, unkempt hair lying on his head in an absolute mess-but somehow it was still charming. His green eyes shone in the dull grey light of the morning sky. His nose bent slightly to the left.

"It sure is. I want to get moving as soon as possible. I wish to bear the mark of a soldier no longer." I replied.

"Hey I hear ya, all this combat keeps me down and depressed. I've felt this way for far too long." he sighed, looking listlessly out at the river.

There was a brief pause, but as I opened my mouth to say something, his head snapped back and his smiling face returned.

"Well there's no use in worrying. It'll all be over soon." he reassured me.

"Not exactly. Being a soldier will be over soon, not all of it." I countered slyly.

"Oh don't get all technical on me. You know what I mean." he grinned.

He looked back out at the river, his face was now pining for something.

"I know that just being a soldier will be over, but for me, it also signifies a new beginning. Hard to believe that it will all be ending soon. Everything I've experienced here will come to a screeching halt. A new chapter can finally begin." His voice was soft but somehow echoed out in yearning. The shine in his eyes grew precocious, glinting with determination.

"You must have suffered a hell of a lot during your time here." I said. The tone of my voice trying to indicate to him understanding. My heart filled with empathy and compassion the longer I spent looking at him. Sitting before me was someone who very much felt the wounds of bloodshed forcefully daggered into his spirit. This man was someone I finally could relate to, at least in the most obvious and explicit sense.

"Yeah it's been tough to say the least." he laughed dryly. "But there is a silver lining. Reminding myself of it has helped me to face the daily damnation of this war."

I looked at him, my eyes squinting, puzzled by this statement. The good from this war he apparently alluded to was beyond me.

"I'm not sure what you mean. What exactly is the silver lining here?" I ventured.

"All the good we have done for others. All the values and ideas we have fought for. Our actions as protectors and defenders of the innocent. Knowing that what I've done has kept people safe from harm is my most comforting thought." he said meekly.

I sat there in astonishment. Not quite believing the words my ears had just processed. Dread began creeping through my body once more. Yet another one of these army men who believed in the cause. Once again I would have to tread with apprehension. Once again I would have to react carefully and succinctly in order to please him.

No.

I'm tired of this. Of putting up with all of it. This glorification of war and these false narratives of heroism. Now's as good a time as any to fight against these delusions. I can tell that this man has goodness in him in spite of his misguidance. He has the right intentions. He is not one to feign innocence. I will not let him fall prey to this propaganda that's been ceaselessly fed to us.

"The good we have done? Protecting the innocent? What innocent people have we protected? All we've done is sit stuck in no man's land, firing off round after round at a faceless enemy. Never once reaching an end goal. Never once gaining any kind of result. Our tour has ended, and we all have suffered for nothing."

I allowed that to sink in for a moment.

"Well, we're putting a stop to any threats or dangers before they arrive. We fight so it doesn't get to a point where the innocent are harmed." he replied earnestly. "We have the fight over here in order to protect what's back at home."

"But innocent people have already become victims of this conflict. You saw the results of that raid as we passed it by not too long ago, did you not?" I asked sternly.

"It's only because troops weren't there," he said. "Those people didn't have anyone to protect them. Of course there should've been, but we do what we can."

"Ah, so that's all there is to it. If legions of people die what can we do, right? What about those values and ideals that we supposedly fight for? What is it of those that makes it so important to fight for them?" I challenged.

"We fight for freedom. Freedom for all those who cannot fight for themselves. The idea that everyone can and should be free. What? Do you not believe that is the case?" he snapped back.

"Oh please, give me a break. That's common sense. That's the most basic, most fundamental ideal to have. No one plain and simply disagrees with that sentiment. The ones who sent us off to war in the first place, they tell us this all the time. They constantly reinforce this idea as we ceaselessly fight. But what me and you have gone through; what we have actually seen, what has happened within this war, makes this painfully and obviously not the case. We gained no ground. We never conquered or protected or saved anything. These warmongers have lied to us. And they will continue lying to us until they get what they desire." I declared.

"And what is their desire?" he asked, this time much more quietly.

"To conquer what they fear. To conquer it at any cost. What lies within them is a fear far different from that of you or me." I said.

"What kind of fear is it?"

"The cowards kind."

I was met with silence. All traces of a smile were wiped from his face. In its place was a stone cold hardness that I almost couldn't fathom. I found it hard to believe that the man could even make such an expression. A pin dropping would do no good in addressing the stillness that radiated between us.

I looked at him carefully, feeling anguish; almost regretful that it had come to this. I inhaled sharply.

"Who have we been fighting for all this time?"

The entire universe came to a halt as that question left my lips. I could feel the eons passing as I sat on that train. What I sensed in the air could hardly be described as tension. Tension would indicate some kind of a struggle. Something coming to a breaking point. Instead I felt as if I had witnessed all of life flashing before my eyes. The question I asked began shifting; mutating into a kaleidoscopic time-lapse of every living creature. Each and every shard of glass was racing towards an end, ready to be forgotten in the blink of an eye. But in that same blink the shards were replaced. Always primed to move on to the next living thing. I realized something at that moment. That in these last few years, I never once asked myself this question. Of course I could provide a technical answer of what forces and powers that be which sent us off, but I never reflected on it. A day ago this question filled me with nothing but fury, and this fury had not allowed me to see straight. But as I sit now and think, the question has quickly become impenetrable. I am dumbstruck by its sheer mystery, and it was no different for this young man sitting before me. Even in the face of all this suffering I am still nothing but a small blemish on the face of the universe. I am the blind leading the blind. To believe I possessed some special knowledge or insight is comical, really. I thought the ordeal of war had made me enlightened on the nature of being, but I remain as foolish as I ever was.

I couldn't help it, I began to laugh. I laughed harder than I ever had before. A sunken, hollow laugh that was filled to the brim with cynicism. The space I occupied became far more immense and monstrous. Still I laughed, almost as if in protest.

As I sat there laughing, the man behind me cracked a smile. I'm ashamed to say it made me pleased. I had successfully rallied one ally to my side. One that could join me in all my pretentious beliefs. At last I had found a connection, and what a connection it was.

But as my laughter died down and I got my bearings, I took a closer look at my new compatriot. I looked once again at his expression.

Something was horribly wrong.

Resting on the man's face was the most blood-curdling configuration of wrinkles I had ever seen. The corners of his mouth had become suspended by puppet strings. I could see every tooth. They shined with a white glint filled with emptiness. The lips and gums were spread wide, straining under all the pressure. The skin was shriveled up, spoiled, rotten. In his eyes was desperation. A sick desperation. His lower lip began to quiver. His clenched fists trembled. I recoiled, pressing up against the car window; unable to move.

This young man; who was filled to the brim with deep thoughtfulness, who had unrelenting optimism, who had yearned and dreamed of being virtuous in the face of all this terror, picked up his rifle.

In one fluid motion, he shattered the glass window next to him, climbed out onto the tracks, and threw himself into the river.

I watched as his body floated away with the current, his blood making trails in the water.

My eyes swam with tears.

I was met without a single reaction. Nobody in the car attempted to say or do anything. No one else seemed to care.

The train whistle blew. We slowly started chugging along. The engine was back up and running.

Act Two:

34

1.

We are finally here.

It's wildly outlandish seeing this base again. Even though physically I'm in this place, I'm still waiting for it to sink in. It feels so surreal that I had almost forgotten what it looked like. But as I stepped off the train and into the station, soon enough it all came back to me. As I take in my surroundings, a soothing calm washes over the whole of my body. For a brief moment I became so relaxed as to amble along, making sure to drink in my final day here-taking one massive, prolonged sip after another. As my head turns round and round, my eyes catch glimpses of very familiar sights. Most of them I'd soon like to forget.

In the heart of the base stood the dining hall in which I'd spent countless days with a table all to myself. Safe in a microcosm of my own design. Standing next to it was the post office. I can't remember if I ever sent any letters. I wonder if there are any letters for me? I should check and make sure when I have the time. Peering out past these few buildings, I see off in the distance the training grounds. My old training grounds. The place where my body was grinded down and built back up. Achieving after many months what people consider the ideal physiological archetype. I suppose that's one tangible change I got out of all this.

These grounds soon give way to the base's one and only lake and the isle of sand that accompanies it. This still remains the area of the base most unfamiliar to me. Many of the soldiers here chose the lake as a means to occupy their down time, but I was not one of them. I never once had felt the sand between my toes or the cool water lapping at my feet. I looked down the road I was walking. At the road's end is a landing strip with several fighter jets parked on its surface. I noticed that there are fewer of them now than when I'd left. Turning to face the side of the road, the old holey chapel looms over me, its weathered cross bared on the door like a set of rotting teeth; but as I walked it quickly got interrupted. For on either side of me sitting row to row were the dwelling places of the commandants, every building lined in a cold, logical symmetry.

The calm and ease I'd felt when I stepped off the train has now all but vanished.

As I and the rest of my unit made our way back to the barracks, I could sense the presence of a force so wicked and corrupt that my heart began to palpitate. There were an uncountable amount of eyes in this place. All of them coming to rest upon me. The pressure of these eyes proved too much, I felt as if I was suffocating in this little strip where their houses lie. But just when I couldn't bear it any longer, the corridor ended. The barracks were just a stone's throw away.

Finally, we arrived back at our sleeping quarters. Many sighs of relief were let loose. We were forced to sleep on those cold, hard and dirty mattress pads no longer. My bunkmate had managed to sneak in a few handles of liquor from the train, one of which they were gracious enough to lend me. Lying in that bed for the first time in so long, I forced myself to take a pause in the stillness-even if only for a little while.

Suddenly several hours had passed, and I was woken by the dinner bell.

I sit at my own table, my own little microcosm, for the final time. I am beholden to this great hall and the mechanisms which keep it functioning. Such a grand and eloquent place designed for the purpose of fueling murderers. No doubt in my mind that it was a worthwhile investment.

Cutting through all the hustle and chatter and commotion, there rang out the sound of silverware striking against glass. The noise which reverberated throughout the hall rapidly died down. Standing front and center at the source of the ringing was the base commander. Every feature and shape on her face was so plain that I'd forgotten what it was she looked like. As she surveyed the room, she smiled an eerie smile, one that I was all too familiar with. The difference this time was the intent behind it. This smile contained nothing really. What it conveyed wasn't any human emotion at all. At least none that I could think of. It was the object of pure unfeeling. It was devoid of anything. How anyone could manage to make such an expression, without any strain and with full sincerity, is beyond me. Maintaining this smile she took a breath.

"Hello everyone and welcome to your final meal at The Military Base!!!" her voice booming.

Resounding cheers traveled back in response.

"Are all of you ready to finally get out of here?" she asked. Snickering ever so slightly as she said it.

Again, there were cheers.

"I know that this tour of yours has been a long and arduous one. Many of you have come back with scars, the likes of which you will carry along for the rest of your life." her sullen tone reeked of insincerity. The words came out hollow.

A quiet hush fell over the hall. From outside the muffled sounds of crickets and cicadas weaved to and fro. Humming together in peaceful morbidity.

"As many of you may know already, this war is far from over. There is still much work to be done." she said firmly, the smile removing itself for a moment.

A scattered series of whispers and murmurs ensued.

However it quickly returned, "But that's not for you all to worry about, rest assured. After today, you will be reunited with your families and loved ones. With those you haven't seen in such a long time. Look forward to tomorrow and every day after, for your fight is finally over." her fist raised up in triumph.

Cheering again, this time with rounds and rounds of applause accompanying it.

"Thank you all so incredibly much for your service. It honors us that you chose to be a part of this cause. We are eternally grateful. The hall is all you can eat tonight, so make sure you dig in!" she shouted.

As she said this, everyone in the hall got up, excitedly rushing and swarming to the buffet tables like bees. Something new and unknown for all of us was waiting just over the horizon. What was in that hall I could only describe as the indomitability of the human spirit. Each and every person here was destined to triumph, even me.

Watching this all unfold, my eyes began to twinkle.

As night falls, I head over to the post office to see if maybe any letters have been left for me. I'm not expecting anything. Why would I? After all, I don't believe I ever wrote to anyone after I left, but I'll check just in case.

I slip inside, searching for the mailroom. I find it and open the door, feeling unusually more tense than I should. I begin to look for my division, then my unit, then my name.

The mail slot is empty, save for some specks of dust.

I expected this, you can't not write to someone and anticipate a response. Not a big deal. Someone will be waiting for me tomorrow either way. I've always preferred face to face contact to begin with.

I am forced to once again pass that chapel and those officers' houses. The quiet unease I felt when I first arrived returns when I enter this strip. As I make my way through, I notice that many lights are still illuminated. Hovering from above and shining down onto the street. I shiver thinking about the things they might be putting into motion.

I wonder which unfortunate souls are next in line to suffer.

Even after getting safely back into my bunk, the fear still remains. It takes a while for me to shut my eyes. Once I drift off to sleep, I'm haunted by my dreams. Are these even dreams? Maybe they're just memories... I've reached a point in my conditioning where I cannot tell the difference.

As I sleep, I see visions of the war. Although I don't think they are just visions of my war. No, what I see is totality. A sum product of all its anguish. Silently, I watch lines of toy soldiers practice handling their firearms. They march off, eyes glazing over as they chant in uniform. Cars and buildings are lit ablaze. The destruction forces people underground. There are sewers muddied with hundreds of civilians. Mothers clutching babies. Missing limbs that force many of these same civilians to crawl through the sludge. Dragging themselves by a single appendage if they have to. A soldier with a bullet going through their head, dying instantaneously. A father executed in front of his son. A son executed in front of his father.

In the midst of all of it, a seer sits perched on a high tower shrouded in darkness. Putting a stop to none of it. Never once interfering. Just watching, listening, waiting.

What was all of this for? Tell me what oh so noble cause demands that we as human beings behave this way. Not a single thing on this earth, material or otherwise, warrants this. It's unfathomable. But this is what we're taught. That it is entirely necessary in order to defend and to protect. Am I supposed to believe that this is human nature? That this is what it must come to? Suddenly their silence breaks. The seer stops and laughs. Laughs in the face of all this glorious absurdity. All at once they've been reduced to nothing more than a fool. A jester clawing at its face as the madness ensues. The jester looks wretchedly around for their king, but there is no king. There never was to begin with. You feel that you must scream but you can't. The only sound you're able to produce is laughter. So you laugh. Laugh into the echo of oblivion. This show, this performance we are in is the cruelest comedy of all. One that is entirely preventable. A disparity that we continue to allow, no matter how many times history warns us of it. This is the definition of insanity.

There are things that we invent and make-up, completely fabricated. Rooted entirely in our own imaginations.

And because of these things, people have to die.

It was true all along. God stays in heaven in order to keep away from us. He didn't damn anything. We damned ourselves.

Something grazed against my leg. Something almost too gentle.

I opened my eyes and abruptly found myself standing in the middle of a field. I had no bearing on my surroundings and no clue as to my location, but I didn't panic. I didn't feel disoriented. In fact I didn't react in any way at all. I just stood there in a daze, engulfed in a cloud of listlessness. The only thing I could sense was the wind pushing and pulling tall stocks of grass against my body. I could see all around for miles and miles. I turned slowly, carefully surveying where I was at that point in space and time. Off in the distance some ways away, I saw the red and white blinking lights that emanated from the base. I thought that I may have been on its outskirts, but I realized now I was much farther than that. I don't even want to question what spurred me to come this far. All I have ahead of me is the long and strenuous journey back.

I gathered myself, and took the first of many steps back towards the base.

This is the last time I will ever be heading towards it. The realization fills me with an indescribable amount of satisfaction. I find it impossible to restrain myself. I howl in celebration, letting the sound be carried onward by the night wind. I allow myself to become enveloped wholly in selfishness. A selfishness I have well earned.

Hope is awakening within me again. This time more intensely and acute than it ever has before. I feel as if I can't wait any longer, like I'm about to break open hope's door myself and simply walk in. With each passing step I'm finding it harder and harder to contain my excitement. It's all spilling out of me in an abundance I can barely control. I'm close, so incredibly close to seeing all these people again. Parents, friends, relatives, anyone else that pops in my head. Anybody I could possibly think of. I ruminate about what might happen, contemplating all the possible scenarios in my mind. Making careful deliberations about what I will say and how I'm going to say it. I became lost in these thoughts, so lost that I hadn't even noticed I was walking on the road back to the barracks. I had even passed by the chapel and officers houses without any alarm. I had been so enraptured in dreaming about tomorrow that I became immune to the fear those buildings tried to impose on me. When I reached the sleeping quarters and sat down on my bed, my right leg started bouncing. I never went back to sleep. I couldn't.

Soon enough the roosters crowed.

An hour passes, two, then three. At this point I'm just about ready to jump out of my skin. I feel like a dog, completely manic and frenzied in my excitement. Panting with my tongue hanging out. Tail wagging at a bullets pace. It's strange, allowing myself to sink so deeply into the eagerness of seeing another person. Not questioning the bizarre nature of human connectivity. The lower I sink the more I want out of this undefinable obscurity. All its mystery and excitement. The piercing, amaranthine beauty of it. I want to take this journey for the first time in my life. Experience bonds and connections like I never have before. The gentle embrace from an old, familiar acquaintance. The ease and comfort that is being with family. The safety and security it provides. A special kind of relationship shared with a group of people regardless of blood or lineage or some other biological factor. Being with friends. All of the spontaneous ordeals we'll get to look back on and fondly remember. Laughing all of our troubles away as we carry on into the night. I want to hold someone's hand. I want to wake up every morning next to them. To look into their softly smiling face as light pours gently in from the window. To bring them into my arms and feel their warmth.

Love.

I want to love. To lift others up in any way that I can. To feel a universe shattering intensity for other people. To be able to shake the stars themselves with my spirit. I know this to be true. That's what I was put on this earth for. Overly sentimental as it may be, I understand now. That is what it means to live. I could feel my heart burning with benevolence.

A tap on my shoulder causes me to look up. My bunkmate is standing there looking down at me, completely dumbstruck. In awe.

"Yknow, I don't think I've ever seen you smile before." they said with amazement.

I hadn't even noticed, "Some things have changed." I said. This time with a renewed vigor. Vigor I believed to not exist.

"Well I'm glad, I really am." they said, smiling back at me. Picking up their bags, they headed out to exit as everyone else continued to pack up.

Gathering up my belongings, I come across many things that remind me of my past life outside of the war. I'd forgotten I'd even had one. Seeing these things after so long I was suddenly wistful, almost succumbing to regret, but I knew I couldn't look at them in that way. These items are those which remind me of who I am, represent a return to normalcy. A newfound knowledge I will bring with me into the rest of my days. I put my hands up to my heart, feeling its newfound warmth. It's beating calm and serene. As I traced along the left side of my chest, I was interrupted by the cold, hard bronze medallion that I'd forgotten to take off. I quickly recoiled, immediately removing the pin and placing the medal in my breast pocket. I'll deal with it later. All my bags are packed and ready to go. Pickups are bound to happen any minute now.

With that, I set out into a new day. In stride alongside the rest of the troops.

It was quite dense and crowded when I arrived. All kinds of people from all over had come to take their soldiers home. It was the happiest congregation of people I had ever witnessed. The sun was warm. The breeze was blowing gently. I could not have asked for more perfect conditions. I plunged directly into the heart of the crowd, waiting for a familiar face. Any minute now.

A man with so much life still left to live falls into the embrace of teary eyed parents. A father reunites with his daughter, in disbelief at how much she's grown. Realizing how much he has missed, he vows to always stay by her side. A mother squeezes her son so tightly, refusing to ever let go. Swearing up and down that she will never let him leave for war again.

Ten minutes pass.

An excited and emotional group of friends gather around their soldier, almost collapsing under the weight of the largest group hug I've ever seen. A young couple collides after so long apart, twirling round and round in each other's arms. With tears and love-sick sighs, their cheeks nuzzle against one another. A pit forms at the bottom of my stomach as I watch this. My chest tightens.

Twenty minutes pass.

The crowd is starting to grow thin, and I am starting to grow more desperate. My head spins in every direction as I frantically search for someone, anyone, to approach me. My breaths are becoming shorter, heavier.

Thirty Minutes have passed.

Here I stand staring down at my own two feet. Averting my eyes so that maybe, just maybe, I'll hear a voice call out my name. I'll be caught by surprise just as I give up. Given some consolation. Some reprieve. I look up. It is now completely empty save for myself.

No one came for me.

I had entered the house of hope, scouring every part of it. Searching high and low. Checking every nook and cranny, every element to its framework-only to find that everyone was gone. There wasn't a single trace of them left. Nobody lived here to begin with.

A familiar, overpowering numbness has returned. Everything in my vision has grown dim. The day is done. I have grown useful for nothing more than pointless meandering. What is left for me to do? Where am I to go now? All of this waiting and waiting, still I remain outside humankind. Still my circumstances remain unchanged. I have been reduced to a mere tumbleweed, blowing into view every once in a while. Only taken into account since the rest of the town is empty and nothing else moves. I am still stuck in this goddamned base, this time with no way out. Even if I were to make it out of here on my own, I have no idea where I'd be or where I'd end up. I would become lost in the physical sense. That's another worry I do not need at the moment.

The air has grown quiet, the only sound remaining being the voice of the base mocking me. "Why are you still here?" its voice filled with contempt. I am now at my barest essentials. A burden. Will they send me back to fight? Will I become witness to the horrors of battle all over again?

The night has come again to engulf me. My head is swimming with dread. I'm beginning to lose all the sense I have left. My mind needs to be cleared, it needs to be cleansed.

The liquor. I still have the liquor sitting in my trunk.

I sat on the side of my bed, shooting down as much as I could before I got sick. I puked, paused for a moment to catch my breath, then downed some more. From the wall next to me, a fragmented glow poured in through the window-casting luminescence against the hard grey floor. My body, hunched over and wretched, hobbled into that cold, pale moonlight. My face shriveled up as the light beamed down. Basking in its stiffness and dispassion, joined together in singularity.

There's nowhere for me to go anymore. Nothing for me to work towards. No more purpose to strive for. Weighing all of my options, none of it will suffice. My only outcome is being deployed to become cannon fodder once more. By then I'll have become a statistic. Either that or I escape to wander aimlessly for the rest of my life. Repeating over and over these choices in my head, I realize now what a disgraceful existence either would be to lead. In shame and humiliation I am buried.

I decided I was going to drown myself.

The Lake. I had never visited its waters before, and now I can. I can submerge myself in that pool like so many others before me. Go for a light swim, maybe complete some laps. Splash around all idyllic and carefree like. What's even better is I won't have to come out. I'll never have to come out ever again. That sweet, cold darkness will swallow me. For eternity I will feel no pain. I've had enough of all this trying. Trying is what keeps me stuck behind these walls, inadvertently trapped from all my effort. Now, all my wants and wishes will vanish, and with them my miseries shall cease.

I fly out into the night, my legs burning. Arms rocking back and forth on the hinges of my shoulders. I dart past those looming officer quarters and that chapel. I am afraid of them no longer. Where I am going no one will be able to get me. Crossing over to the other side of the base, I quickly pass the dining hall. There is no longer the need to eat. As I come across the post office, I make sure to leave all my worries behind. Worries that no one will ever unearth. Soon enough I find myself on the training grounds, bolting across the vastness of its pasture. A speck of dust that's fallen into the eye of the world.

I'm almost there. The stars are suspended high above the earth. The wind is roaring against my face and out into the air. The moon has come to lead me to your door, my precious Lake. And I finally see, you welcome me with open arms. You are unfeeling, soulless, perfect. You pass no judgment. You can protect me, make sure no one will find me. I feel your grains of sand between my toes, cushioning softly the pads of my feet. What a delightful gift of the senses you have given me. If only I could feel your beach for longer, but there is no more time able to be delayed. All of it has been drained from me. Even the little droplets are beginning to dissipate. Being replaced by the droplets of your shore.

Your foaming, sizzling sea is just out of arm's reach. I can almost taste the salt in the air. I see for the first time your true shape, your true endlessness. You are no mere lake, you are all the oceans. You are all the infinite depths that have ever come to be. I see you, my sweet Lake. I see you. And I know that you see me too. You have been gracious enough to heal me of my afflictions. I am forever yours in return. My feet make contact, and at their base the water is lapping.

lapping

lapping lapping

lapping lapping lapping lapping

lapping lapping lapping lapping lapping lapping lapping lapping
lapping lapping lap

ping lapping

lapping lapping lapping lapping lapping lapping lapping lapping
lapping lapping
lapping lapping lapping lapping lapping lapping lapping lapping
lapping lapping
lapping lapping lapping lapping lapping lapping lapping lapping
lapping lapping
lapping lapping lapping lapping lapping lapping lapping lapping
lapping lapping
lapping lapping lapping lapping lapping lapping lapping lapping
lapping lapping

lapping lapping lapping lapping lapping lapping lapping lapping
lapping lapping
lapping lapping lapping lapping lapping lapping lapping lapping
lapping lapping
lapping lapping lapping lapping lapping lapping lapping lapping
lapping lapping
lapping lapping lapping lapping lapping lapping lapping lapping
lapping lapping
lapping lapping lapping lapping lapping lapping lapping lapping
lapping lapping
lapping lapping lapping lapping lapping lapping lapping lapping
lapping lapping
lapping lapping lapping lapping lapping lapping lapping lapping
lapping lapping
lapping lapping lapping lapping lapping lapping lapping lapping
lapping lapping
lapping lapping lapping lapping lapping lapping lapping lapping
lapping lapping
lapping lapping lapping lapping lapping lapping lapping lapping
lapping lapping

lapping lapping lapping lapping lapping lapping lapping lapping
lapping lapping

lapping lapping lapping lapping lapping lapping lapping lapping
lapping lapping

lapping lapping lapping lapping lapping lapping lapping lapping
lapping lapping

lapping lapping lapping lapping lapping lapping lapping lapping
lapping lapping

lapping lapping lapping lapping lapping lapping lapping lapping
lapping lapping

lapping lapping lapping lapping lapping lapping lapping lapping
lapping lapping

lapping lapping lapping lapping lapping lapping lapping lapping
lapping lapping

lapping lapping lapping lapping lapping lapping lapping lapping
lapping lapping

lapping lapping lapping lapping lapping lapping lapping lapping
lapping lapping

lapping lapping lapping lapping lapping lapping lapping lapping
lapping lapping

lapping lapping lapping lapping lapping lapping lapping lapping
lapping lapping

lapping lapping lapping lapping lapping lapping lapping lapping
lapping lapping

lapping lapping lapping lapping lapping lapping lapping lapping
lapping lapping

lapping lapping lapping lapping lapping lapping lapping lapping
lapping lapping

lapping lapping lapping lapping lapping lapping lapping lapping
lapping lapping
lapping lapping lapping lapping lapping lapping lapping lapping
lapping lapping
lapping lapping lapping lapping lapping lapping lapping lapping
lapping lapping
lapping lapping lapping lapping lapping lapping lapping lapping
lapping lapping
lapping lapping lapping lapping lapping lapping lapping lapping
lapping lapping
lapping lapping lapping lapping lapping lapping lapping lapping
lapping lapping
lapping lapping lapping lapping lapping lapping lapping lapping
lapping lapping
lapping lapping lapping lapping lapping lapping lapping lapping
lapping lapping lapping lapping lapping lapping lapping lapping
lapping lapping lapping lapping
lapping lapping lapping lapping lapping lapping lapping lapping
lapping lapping
lapping lapping lapping lapping lapping lapping lapping lapping
lapping lapping
lapping lapping lapping lapping lapping lapping lapping lapping
lapping lapping
lapping lapping lapping lapping lapping lapping lapping lapping
lapping lapping
lapping lapping lapping lapping lapping lapping lapping lapping
lapping lapping
lapping lapping lapping lapping lapping lapping lapping lapping
lapping lapping

lapping lapping lapping lapping lapping lapping lapping lapping lapping lapping

lapping lapping lapping lapping lapping lapping lapping lapping lapping lapping

lapping lapping lapping lapping lapping lapping lapping lapping
lapping lapping
lapping lapping lapping lapping lapping lapping lapping lapping
lapping lapping
lapping lapping lapping lapping lapping lapping lapping lapping
lapping lapping
lapping lapping lapping lapping lapping lapping lapping lapping
lapping lapping
lapping lapping lapping lapping lapping lapping lapping lapping
lapping lapping
lapping lapping lapping lapping lapping lapping lapping lapping
lapping lapping
lapping lapping lapping lapping lapping lapping lapping lapping
lapping lapping
lapping lapping lapping lapping lapping lapping lapping lapping
lapping lapping
lapping lapping lapping lapping lapping lapping lapping lapping
lapping lapping
lapping lapping lapping lapping lapping lapping lapping lapping
lapping lapping
lapping lapping lapping lapping lapping lapping lapping lapping
lapping lapping
lapping lapping lapping lapping lapping lapping lapping lapping
lapping lapping lapping lapping lapping lapping lapping lapping
lapping lapping lapping lapping
lapping lapping lapping lapping lapping lapping lapping lapping
lapping lapping
lapping lapping lapping lapping lapping lapping lapping lapping
lapping lapping

lapping lapping lapping lapping lapping lapping lapping lapping lapping lapping

lapping lapping lapping lapping lapping lapping lapping lapping lapping lapping

lapping lapping lapping lapping lapping lapping lapping lapping lapping lapping

lapping lapping lapping lapping lapping lapping lapping lapping lapping lapping

lapping lapping lapping lapping lapping lapping lapping lapping lapping lapping lapping lapping lapping lapping lapping lapping lapping lapping lapping

lapping lapping lapping lapping lapping lapping lapping lapping
lapping lapping
lapping lapping lapping lapping lapping lapping lapping lapping
lapping lapping
lapping lapping lapping lapping lapping lapping lapping lapping
lapping lapping
lapping lapping lapping lapping lapping lapping lapping lapping
lapping lapping lapping lapping lapping lapping lapping lapping
lapping lapping lapping lapping
lapping lapping lapping lapping lapping lapping lapping lapping
lapping lapping
lapping lapping lapping lapping lapping lapping lapping lapping
lapping lapping
lapping lapping lapping lapping lapping lapping lapping lapping
lapping lapping
lapping lapping lapping lapping lapping lapping lapping lapping
lapping lapping
lapping lapping lapping lapping lapping lapping lapping lapping
lapping lapping lapping lapping lapping lapping lapping lapping
lapping lapping lapping lapping
lapping lapping lapping lapping lapping lapping lapping lapping
lapping lapping
lapping lapping lapping lapping lapping lapping lapping lapping
lapping lapping
lapping lapping lapping lapping lapping lapping lapping lapping
lapping lapping
lapping lapping lapping lapping lapping lapping lapping lapping
lapping lapping lapping lapping lapping lapping lapping lapping
lapping lapping lapping lapping

lapping lapping lapping lapping lapping lapping lapping lapping
lapping lapping

lapping lapping lapping lapping lapping lapping lapping lapping
lapping lapping

lapping lapping lapping lapping lapping lapping lapping lapping
lapping lapping

lapping lapping lapping lapping lapping lapping lapping lapping
lapping lapping

lapping lapping lapping lapping lapping lapping lapping lapping
lapping lapping lapping lapping lapping lapping lapping lapping
lapping lapping lapping lapping

lapping lapping lapping lapping lapping lapping lapping lapping
lapping lapping lapping lapping lapping lapping lapping lapping
lapping lapping lapping lapping

lapping lapping lapping lapping lapping lapping lapping lapping
lapping lapping

lapping lapping lapping lapping lapping lapping lapping lapping
lapping lapping

lapping lapping lapping lapping lapping lapping lapping lapping
lapping lapping

lapping lapping lapping lapping lapping lapping lapping lapping
lapping lapping

lapping lapping lapping lapping lapping lapping lapping lapping
lapping lapping

lapping lapping lapping lapping lapping lapping lapping lapping
lapping lapping

lapping lapping lapping lapping lapping lapping lapping lapping
lapping lapping

lapping lapping lapping lapping lapping lapping lapping lapping lapping lapping lapping lapping lapping lapping lapping lapping lapping lapping lapping lapping

lapping lapping lapping lapping lapping lapping lapping lapping lapping lapping

lapping lapping lapping lapping lapping lapping lapping lapping lapping lapping

lapping lapping lapping lapping lapping lapping lapping lapping lapping lapping

lapping lapping lapping lapping lapping lapping lapping lapping lapping lapping

lapping lapping lapping lapping lapping lapping lapping lapping lapping lapping

lapping lapping

lapping lapping lapping lapping lapping lapping lapping lapping lapping lapping

lapping lapping lapping lapping lapping lapping lapping lapping lapping lapping

lapping lapping lapping lapping lapping lapping lapping lapping lapping lapping

lapping lapping

lapping lapping lapping lapping lapping lapping lapping lapping lapping lapping

lapping lapping lapping lapping lapping lapping lapping lapping lapping lapping

lapping lapping lapping lapping lapping lapping lapping lapping lapping lapping

lapping lapping lapping lapping lapping lapping lapping lapping lapping lapping

lapping lapping lapping lapping lapping lapping lapping lapping lapping lapping lapping lapping lapping lapping lapping lapping lapping lapping lapping lapping

lapping lapping lapping lapping lapping lapping lapping lapping lapping lapping lapping lapping lapping lapping lapping lapping lapping lapping lapping lapping

lapping lapping lapping lapping lapping lapping lapping lapping lapping lapping

lapping lapping lapping lapping lapping lapping lapping lapping lapping lapping

lapping lapping lapping lapping lapping lapping lapping lapping lapping lapping

lapping lapping lapping lapping lapping lapping lapping lapping lapping lapping

lapping lapping lapping lapping lapping lapping lapping lapping lapping lapping

lapping lapping lapping lapping lapping lapping lapping lapping lapping lapping

lapping lapping lapping lapping lapping lapping lapping lapping lapping lapping

lapping lapping lapping lapping lapping lapping lapping lapping lapping lapping lapping lapping lapping lapping lapping lapping lapping lapping lapping lapping

lapping lapping lapping lapping lapping lapping lapping lapping lapping lapping

lapping lapping lapping lapping lapping lapping lapping lapping lapping lapping

lapping lapping lapping lapping lapping lapping lapping lapping lapping lapping

lapping lapping lapping lapping lapping lapping lapping lapping lapping lapping

lapping lapping lapping lapping lapping lapping lapping lapping lapping lapping

lapping lapping

lapping lapping lapping lapping lapping lapping lapping lapping lapping lapping

lapping lapping lapping lapping lapping lapping lapping lapping lapping lapping

lapping lapping lapping lapping lapping lapping lapping lapping lapping lapping

lapping lapping

lapping lapping lapping lapping lapping lapping lapping lapping lapping lapping

lapping lapping lapping lapping lapping lapping lapping lapping lapping lapping

lapping lapping lapping lapping lapping lapping lapping lapping lapping lapping

lapping lapping lapping lapping lapping lapping lapping lapping lapping lapping

lapping lapping lapping lapping lapping lapping lapping lapping lapping lapping lapping lapping lapping lapping lapping lapping lapping lapping lapping lapping

lapping lapping lapping lapping lapping lapping lapping lapping lapping lapping lapping lapping lapping lapping lapping lapping lapping lapping lapping lapping

lapping lapping lapping lapping lapping lapping lapping lapping lapping lapping

lapping lapping lapping lapping lapping lapping lapping lapping lapping lapping

lapping lapping lapping lapping lapping lapping lapping lapping lapping lapping

lapping lapping lapping lapping lapping lapping lapping lapping lapping lapping

lapping lapping lapping lapping lapping lapping lapping lapping lapping lapping

lapping lapping lapping lapping lapping lapping lapping lapping lapping lapping

lapping lapping lapping lapping lapping lapping lapping lapping lapping lapping

lapping lapping lapping lapping lapping lapping lapping lapping lapping lapping

lapping lapping

lapping lapping lapping lapping lapping lapping lapping lapping lapping lapping

lapping lapping lapping lapping lapping
lapping lapping lapping lapping lapping
lapping lapping lapping lapping lapping lapping lapping lapping lapping lapping

lapping lapping lapping lapping lapping lapping lapping lapping lapping lapping

lapping lapping lapping lapping lapping lapping lapping lapping lapping lapping

lapping lapping lapping lapping lapping lapping lapping lapping lapping lapping lapping lapping lapping lapping lapping lapping lapping lapping lapping lapping

lapping lapping lapping lapping lapping lapping lapping lapping lapping lapping

lapping lapping lapping lapping lapping lapping lapping lapping lapping lapping

lapping lapping lapping lapping lapping lapping lapping lapping lapping lapping

lapping lapping lapping lapping lapping lapping lapping lapping lapping lapping lapping lapping lapping lapping lapping lapping lapping lapping lapping lapping

lapping lapping lapping lapping lapping lapping lapping lapping lapping lapping

lapping lapping lapping lapping lapping lapping lapping lapping lapping lapping

lapping lapping lapping lapping lapping lapping lapping lapping lapping lapping

lapping lapping lapping lapping lapping lapping lapping lapping lapping lapping

lapping lapping lapping lapping lapping lapping lapping lapping lapping lapping lapping lapping lapping lapping lapping lapping lapping lapping lapping lapping

lapping lapping lapping lapping lapping lapping lapping lapping lapping lapping lapping lapping lapping lapping lapping lapping lapping lapping lapping lapping

lapping lapping lapping lapping lapping lapping lapping lapping lapping lapping

lapping lapping lapping lapping lapping lapping lapping lapping lapping lapping

lapping lapping lapping lapping lapping lapping lapping lapping lapping lapping

lapping lapping lapping lapping lapping lapping lapping lapping lapping lapping

lapping lapping lapping lapping lapping lapping lapping lapping lapping lapping

lapping lapping lapping lapping lapping lapping lapping lapping lapping lapping

lapping lapping lapping lapping lapping lapping lapping lapping lapping lapping

lapping lapping

lapping lapping lapping lapping lapping lapping lapping lapping lapping lapping

lapping lapping lapping lapping lapping lapping lapping lapping lapping lapping

lapping lapping lapping lapping lapping lapping lapping lapping lapping lapping

lapping lapping lapping lapping lapping lapping lapping lapping lapping lapping

lapping lapping lapping lapping lapping lapping lapping lapping lapping lapping

lapping lapping

lapping lapping lapping lapping lapping lapping lapping lapping lapping lapping

lapping lapping lapping lapping lapping lapping lapping lapping lapping lapping

lapping lapping lapping lapping lapping lapping lapping lapping lapping lapping

lapping lapping lapping lapping lapping lapping lapping lapping lapping lapping lapping lapping lapping lapping lapping lapping lapping lapping lapping lapping

lapping lapping lapping lapping lapping lapping lapping lapping lapping lapping

lapping lapping lapping lapping lapping lapping lapping lapping lapping lapping

lapping lapping lapping lapping lapping lapping lapping lapping lapping lapping

lapping lapping lapping lapping lapping lapping lapping lapping lapping lapping

lapping lapping lapping lapping lapping lapping lapping lapping lapping lapping lapping lapping lapping lapping lapping lapping lapping lapping lapping lapping

lapping lapping lapping lapping lapping lapping lapping lapping lapping lapping lapping lapping lapping lapping lapping lapping lapping lapping lapping lapping

lapping lapping lapping lapping lapping lapping lapping lapping lapping lapping

lapping lapping lapping lapping lapping lapping lapping lapping lapping lapping

lapping lapping lapping lapping lapping lapping lapping lapping lapping lapping

lapping lapping lapping lapping lapping lapping lapping lapping lapping lapping

lapping lapping lapping lapping lapping lapping lapping lapping lapping lapping

lapping lapping lapping lapping lapping lapping lapping lapping lapping lapping

lapping lapping lapping lapping lapping lapping lapping lapping lapping lapping

lapping lapping lapping lapping lapping lapping lapping lapping lapping lapping

lapping lapping

lapping lapping lapping lapping lapping lapping lapping lapping lapping lapping

lapping lapping lapping lapping lapping lapping lapping lapping lapping lapping

lapping lapping lapping lapping lapping lapping lapping lapping lapping lapping

lapping lapping lapping lapping lapping lapping lapping lapping lapping lapping

lapping lapping lapping lapping lapping lapping lapping lapping lapping lapping

lapping lapping lapping lapping lapping lapping lapping lapping lapping lapping lapping lapping lapping lapping lapping lapping lapping lapping lapping lapping

lapping lapping lapping lapping lapping lapping lapping lapping lapping lapping

lapping lapping lapping lapping lapping lapping lapping lapping lapping lapping

lapping lapping lapping lapping lapping lapping lapping lapping lapping lapping

lapping lapping lapping lapping lapping lapping lapping lapping lapping lapping lapping lapping lapping lapping lapping lapping lapping lapping lapping lapping

lapping lapping lapping lapping lapping lapping lapping lapping lapping lapping

lapping lapping lapping lapping lapping lapping lapping lapping lapping lapping

lapping lapping lapping lapping lapping lapping lapping lapping lapping lapping

lapping lapping lapping lapping lapping lapping lapping lapping lapping lapping

lapping lapping lapping lapping lapping lapping lapping lapping lapping lapping lapping lapping lapping lapping lapping lapping lapping lapping lapping lapping

lapping lapping

lapping lapping lapping lapping lapping lapping lapping lapping lapping lapping

lapping lapping lapping lapping lapping lapping lapping lapping
lapping lapping
lapping lapping lapping lapping lapping lapping lapping lapping
lapping lapping

lapping lapping lapping lapping lapping lapping lapping lapping
lapping lapping
lapping lapping lapping lapping lapping lapping lapping lapping
lapping lapping

lapping lapping lapping lapping lapping lapping lapping lapping lapping lapping

lapping lapping lapping lapping lapping lapping lapping lapping lapping lapping

lapping lapping lapping lapping lapping lapping lapping lapping lapping lapping

lapping lapping lapping lapping lapping lapping lapping lapping lapping lapping lapping lapping lapping lapping lapping lapping lapping lapping lapping lapping

lapping lapping lapping lapping lapping lapping lapping lapping lapping lapping

lapping lapping lapping lapping lapping lapping lapping lapping lapping lapping

lapping lapping lapping lapping lapping lapping lapping lapping lapping lapping

lapping lapping lapping lapping lapping lapping lapping lapping lapping lapping

lapping lapping lapping lapping lapping lapping lapping lapping lapping lapping

lapping lapping lapping lapping lapping lapping lapping lapping lapping lapping lapping lapping lapping lapping lapping lapping lapping lapping lapping lapping

lapping lapping lapping lapping lapping lapping lapping lapping lapping lapping

lapping lapping lapping lapping lapping lapping lapping lapping lapping lapping

lapping lapping lapping lapping lapping lapping lapping lapping lapping lapping

lapping lapping

lapping lapping lapping lapping lapping lapping lapping lapping lapping lapping

lapping lapping lapping lapping lapping lapping lapping lapping lapping lapping

lapping lapping lapping lapping lapping lapping lapping lapping lapping lapping

lapping lapping lapping lapping lapping lapping lapping lapping lapping lapping

lapping lapping lapping lapping lapping lapping lapping lapping lapping lapping lapping lapping lapping lapping lapping lapping lapping lapping lapping lapping

lapping lapping lapping lapping lapping lapping lapping lapping
lapping lapping lapping lapping lapping lapping lapping lapping
lapping lapping lapping lapping
lapping lapping lapping lapping lapping lapping lapping lapping
lapping lapping
lapping lapping lapping lapping lapping lapping lapping lapping
lapping lapping

lapping lapping lapping lapping lapping lapping lapping lapping lapping lapping

lapping lapping lapping lapping lapping lapping lapping lapping lapping lapping

lapping lapping lapping lapping lapping lapping lapping lapping lapping lapping

lapping lapping lapping lapping lapping lapping lapping lapping lapping lapping

lapping lapping lapping lapping lapping lapping lapping lapping lapping lapping

lapping lapping

lapping lapping lapping lapping lapping lapping lapping lapping lapping lapping

lapping lapping lapping lapping lapping lapping lapping lapping lapping lapping

lapping lapping lapping lapping lapping lapping lapping lapping lapping lapping

lapping lapping lapping lapping lapping lapping lapping lapping lapping lapping

lapping lapping

lapping lapping lapping lapping lapping lapping lapping lapping lapping lapping

lapping lapping lapping lapping lapping lapping lapping lapping lapping lapping

lapping lapping lapping lapping lapping lapping lapping lapping lapping lapping

lapping lapping lapping lapping lapping lapping lapping lapping lapping lapping lapping lapping lapping lapping lapping lapping lapping lapping lapping lapping

lapping lapping lapping lapping lapping lapping lapping lapping lapping lapping

lapping lapping lapping lapping lapping lapping lapping lapping lapping lapping

lapping lapping lapping lapping lapping lapping lapping lapping lapping lapping

lapping lapping lapping lapping lapping lapping lapping lapping lapping lapping

It's cold. It's cold

It's warm

2.

I woke up to the noise of gasping breath rushing into my ears.

A wash of bright, hot light greeted my vision. I could barely keep my eyes open. Squinting and shielding my face, I saw above me ranks and ranks of fluorescent lights that were entirely unlike the light of day. I noticed I was lying down, lying down in bed. But this was not my bed back in the barracks. Everything about it felt foreign. The color of this bed was composed entirely of rigid, unmoving white. I felt something sinking into my arm. I looked up and saw that it was an IV drip tucked inside my vein. I gathered then that I was in a hospital of some kind. I must be in the nursing building here at this wonderful base.

It really is a pity. For just a moment I thought I'd reached some sort of heaven or nirvana or enlightenment. At the very least some kind of ignorance. But I really am alive. I survived somehow. I'm not entirely sure how I feel, or how I'm supposed to feel. At the moment I seemingly lack the basic energy needed to elicit emotion. Even my most fundamental senses are breaking away from me. I can tell that I'm slipping. My body and mind are at odds. Each one vying for control. Not realizing that in order for both to work they must work together. Is this now my eternal state? My true fate? Or could it just be the morphine? I looked down to the end of the bed. There was a stain seeping into the sheets. I pissed myself. I hadn't felt it in the slightest.

I can't really react to any of this. My body is depleted of energy. I have not the strength to move a single muscle even if I wanted to. I resolved that the only possibility was to wait for someone to come. It's all I could stand to do. Regardless of how long it was going to take, I'd be here. This may very well be the only outcome that remains. Being stuck in the same exact spot for god knows how long.

Waiting. A lifetime of waiting.

This could be all I am destined for, but that thought didn't upset me much. If I were to resign myself purely to happenstance, the three fates would make no change to the ways in which they'd spin my thread. I'd be a fool to fight against this. The ways in which I live are out of my hands now.

I heard a faint click to my right, then a shouting voice I could just barely make out. It was being swallowed by the sounds of a helicopter. I turned and noticed the television sitting on the corner wall of the room, its film grainy and discolored. Gazing into it, I saw fire enveloping the streets of a city as buildings crumbled. After that it was just smoke. The voice was yelling something about death tolls and damages. Apparently the enemy had successfully invaded a major city and base of operations we'd held down and fortified. The voice continued on about how this was a somber tragedy and that people needed to be ready for anything.

Suddenly I picked up the sound of rapidly approaching footsteps. A set of double doors just outside my periphery swung open. In hurried a nurse. Her eyes widened when she saw me. Whether from excitement or fear, I wasn't sure.

"You're finally awake!" she exclaimed. Quickly jotting down something on her clipboard. "Honestly, it was up in the air if that ever was going to happen." her laughter filled the air with pity. It sounded more condescending than anything.

"How did I get here?" I managed to ask. Though my words were rather slurred.

"Somebody noticed an unfamiliar sight moving fast out in the training grounds, so they went out and investigated. They saw a pair of shoes without an owner sitting on the sand next to the lake. Shortly after they found you floating in the water." her voice got quieter.

I tried to think of something to say, but couldn't. A disturbing silence began permeating the air. Thousands of thoughts and feelings shared between us passed by, completely unspoken. My eyes met with hers. Staring into them I saw an endless pit of sympathy and kindness I knew I was ill prepared for. It was far more than I deserved.

I managed to feign a smile "Ah, no need to worry about that. It's all over now." I said, barely able to maintain composure.

She shook her head "No it's not. You need time to recover. There's still a lot of water leftover in your lungs that needs to be drained. There's also a concerning lack of oxygen circulating through your body. You'll need to stay here for at least a few days before anything else." her voice grew hard and stern.

"Sure thing" I responded. I was now clinging onto that smile for dear life.

"We still need to run some tests, but the plan is the doctor is going to be in here routinely to drain the fluid from your lungs. There's also this." she reached down beside herself, wheeling forward an oxygen tank.

"You need to be hooked up to this at all times. Only remove it when you need to relieve yourself. The restroom is at the end of this ward." she flicked her head towards its general direction.

"Thank you kindly." I replied in a pseudo sort of earnestness.

The nurse turned her back on me and took her leave. After a few steps she suddenly stopped.

"One more thing." she paused. Her shoulders were rising and falling heavily. I understood then she held enmity towards me. Terrified, I wonder what it is I did wrong. Without even looking at me, she forced me to shrink down further into my bed.

"Don't smile at me again. The least you could do is be sincere."

The door slammed behind her.

She saw right through me. In no time at all she had easily pulled back a piece of the curtain on my lifes performance. Although I'll admit my attempts at a mask were poor to begin with. I could barely control my facial muscles and it was a miracle I managed to do as well as I did. I was wracked with guilt for trying to deceive her, but at the same time I knew I could never fully reveal myself. The nurse knows well enough that I harbor some things. What exactly those things are

I refuse to tell her. I myself lack the energy to stand before that dock. I don't actually care about anything anymore, even trying again what I attempted at the lake. The only thing I want now is to retreat as far away from my mind as possible. I can't strike a balance. Within me is the capacity to either feel everything or nothing at all.

Days allegedly pass, though I can only draw that conclusion because the doctor comes to check on me every six hours or so. At least that's what he told me when he first arrived, but this place isn't so bad. There's a lovely sort of serenity in this mundane ward. It is entirely empty save for me. I can sit with myself. No one else here to pry and interrupt. There is no one watching with their eyes. I have a servant who regularly refills my oxygen tank and one that drains the water from my lungs. In here, I am my own god. I dominate over my own realm, my own reality, with ease.

Outside is a prison.

I think the soldier with the beady black eyes might be right.

Then one day my doctor came back into the ward only an hour after he had left. He pulled up a stool and sat next to me with an honest, genuine grin on his face.

"Very good news. Your oxygen levels are almost entirely back to normal. There's no more fluid in those lungs left to drain. Do you want to try getting up?" he asked.

I sat up and got on my feet effortlessly. I hadn't even felt the sensation that my strength had returned.

"Good. That's very good." he muttered, his head bobbed up and down.

I turned to face him, hiding my disappointment.

"I'll inform the officers that are still here that you're alive and well. They'll want to see you and discuss some things, I'm sure."

"That's nice to hear." I said half-heartedly.

"I'll come and fetch you when they've arrived," said the doctor.

There was nothing more I wanted to say to him. I watched as he fidgeted and squirmed awkwardly in that stool of his.

"Guess I'd better be off." whispering sheepishly, he stood up and left.

Seeing another one of these leaders, let alone multiple, was the last thing I wanted to deal with. But after taking into account an objective view of my situation, I suppose the outcome is inevitable. I thought about it for a moment, trying to escape. However in my foolish thought I'd forgotten there was nowhere to run away to. I'll have to face these warmongers as best I can, readily and determined to steel myself through in order to obtain my only way out.

Many hours must have passed by the time the doctor came back to the ward. He stood in front of the exit, holding the double doors wide open.

"The officers are ready for you downstairs." he said plainly "Follow me ."

The old, rusted elevator groaned in agony on its way down. The lights on the floor panel flashed and burned hot red as we trickled towards the bottom. There was something sinister to this place. An unshakeable eeriness. Had I not known any better, it felt almost certain that we were quickly descending into the lower rings of hell. The elevator door rattled open. The doctor and I stepped out into the lobby.

"They're waiting for you in that conference room over there." he pointed to a door on the left.

It must've been written all over my face how much apprehension I held towards this visit, because right then the doctor gave me a knowing look and said "Good luck" before disappearing down the hall.

Each step towards that door held monumental, immeasurable weight. I was being ever so steadily submerged in fear the closer I got. I was hardly latching on to the handle as I pulled it open.

Sitting at the opposing side of the table were four men up to their britches in medals and badges, reveling in murderous gluttony. One of them was slightly pudgy, with a bald head spotted in freckles. He had a mustache that curled in an unbelievably cartoonish way. Two of them were fairly tall and lanky. Both having a sort of faded buzz cut accompanied by brown eyes. Eyes that more closely resembled a pitbull than a puppy dog. It looked like they were brothers. I'd be surprised if they weren't anyway. When I looked at the last one, I immediately noticed the massive, gashing scar streaking across his cheek. His expression was stone cold and unmoving. I could make out no sign of life anywhere. I understood then that this scar ran far deeper than his cheek. A scar that all of us at war are forced to give sanctum. But I knew the wound he possessed was not something I could resonate with. For he did not fight against the forces that transformed him into this. Instead he chose to become one with the very source of his anguish. A man that hungers for war. Thrives off it. Above all I had to be the most conscious and aware of him. The base commander was here as well. She sat at the end of the table, observing. She had that smile still, that goddamned smile.

"So you're the mysterious, unidentifiable object in the night we've heard so much about." the pudgy one with the freckled head said. "Tell me, how'd you end up in the lake at such an hour?"

I trembled at the idea of giving these masters of war an honest answer. There was nothing about him that would convince me to do so. Whatever I say might be used against me. But I was unsure whether or not any lie I told would be believable. The only way to find out was to try. I offered him my first attempt.

"Well you see, I was taking a nighttime walk. Just getting some fresh air seeing as I was stuck in the barracks all day. I was wandering this way and that, and before I knew it I found myself strolling along the edge of the lake. One misplaced foot caused me to slip and fall into the water. I would've swam, but I never learned how."

This I managed to articulate well enough. Some of it was truthful too. I didn't know how to swim. It's partly why I chose the lake.

The pudgy officer took a sharp breath of air and responded "That's all well and good, but it still doesn't explain the pair of shoes we found on the beachhead. There's no sand to be found anywhere on the lake's perimeter. Why would your shoes be taken off if you didn't plan on going for a swim?"

And just like that, my lie had been broken down and dissected. The other officers sat in silence and watched, knowing they needed to say nothing. Already I'm growing tired of this. They can do what they want with me for all I care. I don't fear these men. I never did. I decided then to go with a different approach.

I didn't say anything. Instead I spent the unkilled time looking down at my feet. It was sweet, that sound. There was nothing I needed to worry about. I should've done this from the start.

"Don't want to answer? That's fine with me." The pudgy officer said. "There's more pressing matters concerning your situation that I'd like to address. The first is in regards to the unit you were placed in. Your tour has ended. You were supposed to leave this base over a week ago. Why didn't you?"

Once again I didn't respond. In fact I haven't stopped looking down at my feet. I unwaveringly maintained the same position.

"The trunk next to your bed has all of your belongings carelessly piled one on top of the other. You made no attempts to leave. This base is not supposed to still be holding you. I'll ask again, why are you still here?"

I held steadfast to my silence and avoidance. I was rooted in it now. I let all the time that needed to pass go right on ahead.

Then the table rattled and shook as the officer with a gaping scar on his cheek slammed his fists against it. He stood up and leaned forward, his chair fell away from him. I looked up. The lack of light in his eyes soon gave way to a bright, scalding anger.

"You heard the man. He's not going to ask again. What are you, a fucking log?! Answer!!!" he roared.

This oh so scary officer truly is inane if he thinks I'm bending to his fury. He's one of the weakest people I've ever met. So fragile in his composure that he's turned this quickly to rage.

Abruptly, this show of force came to an end as one of the tall, lanky ones put a hand on his shoulder. He gave him a cautious look.

The scar cheeked officer was still for a moment. He hesitated as he stood there. Then he let out a sigh. His shoulders loosened and he sat back down.

The lanky officer whose hand had eased this angry beast turned to me and said, "Look, we're all just trying to gain a better understanding of your situation so that we can help. Still being stuck here is the last thing any of us want for you. So please, tell us. Is there anything at all we can do? Any requests? Any friends or family members you'd like us to contact?"

I thought I had protected myself, but right then and there my walls crumbled. I realized then that no one wanted to see me. If they wanted to they would have done so already. For me to reach out would be pointless. This I knew to be the truth.

I brought my hands up to my head, covering my face as best I could. The noise I made then was a soft, warbled gurgling. I sounded like an animal.

To not be wanted means there is something to me that is deeply unpleasant. Something to be avoided whenever possible. At best tolerated.

A hush fell over the room at that moment. I allowed these men and this base commander a small window into my true existence and now, they can exploit whatever they want for their own purposes. I thought I was stronger than this, it seems I was wrong.

"Ok" traveled the voice of the lanky officer from across the table. "We won't press any further questions on you."

I looked up, quite taken aback by this response.

"I'm sure we can arrange something for you. In the meantime, you can stay here as long as you'd like. We'll consider all your options and go from there." said the lanky officer. As he said this he looked around at his compatriots. Nodding and muttering, they begrudgingly agreed. He looked over at the base commander who also nodded. She was still smiling.

"Go back to your bunk for now. We'll update you in the morning." The lanky officer's voice carried a note of finality.

I got up to go, but before I left I began to laugh. It started so suddenly, so uncontrollably, that I couldn't stop. I wiped the tears from my eyes as I straddled that extremely thin line. Who's to say which place they came from? I certainly couldn't tell you.

"Something funny?" the officer with the scar demanded. His tone and demeanor was once again aggressive.

I grinned "Oh nothing, officer. I was just thinking about what an honor it is to serve!"

I left before anyone could respond.

Walking back to the barracks, I sense the breaking point coming soon. I can feel the excess tension in my muscles. It's shaking me all the way down to my roots. I don't trust a single one of them. Sure, that lanky officer was able to spare some sympathy, but at the end of the day I know he is just like the rest of them. I'm a nuisance that needs to be taken care of sooner rather than later. Not only that but a liability as well. They're the ones to take the fall if anything else were to happen to me. What a horrible thing, to be liable for someone. For a relationship to be built, at its very foundation, on responsibility and obligation. Two people sharing at the core of their relationship a burden. The strain that is placed on both parties because they feel they have no other choice. I'd rather have no relationships at all instead of an obligatory commitment.

I looked up into the sky. There was a great ball of fire and smoke which plumed high above everything. Next to it and a little ways away hung the sun. It cast a warm glow that tried to compensate for the destruction, but it was far too late. Its duty to the people of this earth seemed half-hearted then. I wondered why that was.

Despite the meeting being so brief, I feel exhausted. I cannot recall the last time something drained me so quickly and efficiently. The moon isn't out tonight, it's being shrouded by smoke. There's smoke everywhere. I can't see further than a few inches past my hand.

I lower it down gradually. I stare as it goes limp. A few moments later I drift off. It feels as if I am once again back in the water.

When I woke up next. The lanky officer was standing beside me, gazing out the window a dejected kind of gaze. I sat up in my bed. My rustling caused him to turn. His eyes grew soft. He gently smirked upon seeing me.

"How are you feeling?" he asked.

"No different than I was yesterday."

"I see." he said, stroking his chin.

Without further delay he held up the medal of honor I had received "We found this in your army jacket."

I looked questioningly at him as he handed it back to me "Yeah, what about it?"

"It's very rare that people in your position receive these kinds of accolades. Only a handful of soldiers here and there earn a medal. That kind of thing forces us to pay attention. You know what I mean?"

I looked up at him, my face rigid and my jaw clenched.

"The kind of soldier that has one of these is invaluable to us. It means your experience in combat is of the utmost rarity. It will help us in winning thi-"

"If you send me back out to fight, I will kill myself."

The lanky officer inhaled sharply and held up his index finger. He was about to say something, then he looked into my eyes. After about two seconds, that finger came crashing down.

"All right." he sighed "All right. I'll be sure to send you on your way."

Hurriedly rushing away from my bunk, he called back "I'll come for you later."

After a few minutes of sitting docile in my bed, I got up and carried myself to the dining hall. There's a buffet being served for breakfast I think.

I can't take it anymore. Being here, this godforsaken place, is driving me mad. I close my eyes, trying to find somewhere that I can make my sweet escape to. Even when I don't look, this place still scratches and claws at the back of my mind no matter what. I don't know what else I can try. I am mere inches away from losing myself. From pushing past the point of all reason. That wouldn't be so bad, now that I think about it. Perhaps madness is what could give me peace. Could set me free. What comfort is there in reason anyhow? To be a reasonable person is to be a husk, an empty shell of rationality that deteriorates the spirit. Chips away at it, kills it slowly so by the time your life comes to an end, you'll leave a logical and simplistic actor that never really knew anyone. And you'll never be known. Then you're forgotten.

The thing that concerns me more is what I'll do to others with this newfound madness. I have the sense that something bad, something very bad, will occur if I can't keep it at bay. If that happens, there need to be others around who must intervene and stop me. I'll have to be put down like a dog.

I want to be like a dog.

The echo from the door of my sleeping quarters reached to the end of the bunk where I lay, followed by the sound of rapidly approaching footsteps. I got up to face the lanky officer for what would be the final time.

"I've arranged for you to be taken over into the city. I have a friend there who owes me big time. He'll take care of you until you can get back on your feet. There's gonna be a truck here in a few hours to take you there." he gestured towards the pile of belongings at the foot of my bed.

He paused and gave me a long, hard stare.

"You need some serious help." he said, "You know that, right?"

"I appreciate the astute observation." I replied.

His fists clenched, getting ready to prepare a retort. Then they loosened as he exhaled, finally expending the last of his energy on me.

"Just be ready when the truck gets here. I've done all I can for you."

I watched him all the way as he walked out. It took him much longer than last time. Probably because he wasn't in a hurry. I never saw him again.

Oh, great war machine! Your trumpets play a meaningless fanfare! Your harmony is sustained purely out of discord! Every one of your melodies are dissonant! Each instrument twisted and bent from all this malfeasance! Your song gives me anhedonia anytime I hear it played! Your creators have poisoned the pure, innocent well! Corrupted the incorruptible! The unstoppable force has toppled the immovable object! Are you pleased with yourself? Are you content in all your deliberations? Why do all these wonderful things have to die and you still be alive? Why must you continue to persist? I hope you wither away and crumble to dust for an eternity. And I hope before then you are long forgotten.

The truck pulls up to where I stand, its passenger side face to face with me. The window rolls down, revealing at the wheel a gruff and miserly service worker. With one look I could tell he did not get paid for this nearly enough.

"Get in." he grumbled.

I tossed my things into the backseat, climbed up into the shotgun, and without further ado we rode off. To leave that base was the sweetest thing I ever had felt. I choked back on tears of joy.

The driver looked over puzzled, "Something the matter?"

"No." I said, "As a matter of fact, something isn't the matter any longer."

He muttered something indecipherable to himself. I couldn't be bothered to know what it was.

He dropped any and all questions after that.

Act Three:

1.

It's been a month since I first arrived in the city, or has it been a week? Three months? Two years? I can't remember.

I currently live in an apartment that has two bedrooms. My bedroom comes complimentary with a hideously green floral pattern on its walls. There is a mattress and a pillow and some kind of a covering on the bed. The only other object in there being a nightstand sat quietly beside it. The room is a perfect square. There is a living space with nothing but a loveseat and its recliner as a crooked lamp hangs above both. A television sits against the opposing wall, propped up by a cabinet that I am forbidden from looking into. To the side of the living room sits a small island for a kitchen. The only item visible being a fire extinguisher hooked up to the counters wall. We have no tables. The bathroom is consistently grimy and the faucet always leaks. The owner of this place sleeps in the other bedroom which I have hardly seen. I've only ever caught faint glimpses through a brief window as it gets smaller and smaller until the door is completely shut on me. I'm not allowed to go in there either. Though I did notice the room has that same floral pattern.

My benefactor is a brute. When I first arrived he instantly decided he would become my landlord. From that moment on it was decreed there would be a monthly rent fee that I had to meet or else I'd be out on the streets. How I would meet said fee was in my hands and my hands alone. It was staggering how easily he established this power dynamic. He hung the fact that he was giving me shelter over my head in constant reminder. I was determined to survive one day at a time. He was determined to fulfill me, his one and only obligation. Doing so in whatever way he pleased.

Luckily I managed to find some grunt work in order to stave off this threat. Essentially, my daily task simply involves sealing and packaging any item or product that comes through the assembly line. Doing this almost every day for hours on end. That's all that is ever asked of me. I get by perfectly fine day to day. The factory I work at is only a ten minute walk from my landlord's place. The money I get from this little job meets my landlord's sordid fees. I even have some left over to spend anytime and anywhere I'd like. Though I am unsure what to spend it on. I am unsure what it is I do like. The first things to pop into my mind were all bare necessities.

So this is what life is like in the city. In all its towering glory. Whenever things at the factory grow too mundane or I'm stuck in the apartment for too long, I like to wander around with no direction. Doing so in order to experience firsthand the ingenuity of humankind. Find out what exactly a metropolis is meant to be. Much to my disappointment, what I've come to learn isn't really revelatory information. It isn't all that pleasant either. The city is just a jungle that is devoid of color. The people that live in the city are drained of their color as well. Almost as if there lies below the earth a secret, man-made creature which consumes all color from the inhabitants above, turning them numb and empty-the color it takes becoming its fuel, the sustenance it needs to keep growing. Reducing entirely any will to fight. The city, it seems, is just the tip of the iceberg. The scales, the outer armor of that creature. Attempting to stretch its way into heaven but always being out of reach. Yet drawing dangerously ever closer the more advanced it becomes. The tallest buildings and skyscrapers are spears fashioned to kill god, the final obstacle in humanity's conquest. These tall buildings are used for its citizens' demise as well, but only if they so choose. An option that is always kept open. Never encouraged, but kept open. People in the city are always just dismal enough.

I'm certain we've already overcome the obstacle. In fact I think we overcame it long ago. This is the result of innovation. The methodology that is industrialization. We have no more god to conquer so now we have turned to conquering each other. The end all be all of civilization rests on triumph. Triumph over all knowledge. Knowledge that we must gain before anyone else does. Use that knowledge before anyone else can. That is what war is. The final solution. The ultimate end. Once everything that can be known is known, there is nothing else left to do but kill each other.

Thick, dense briars of brick constantly impose on my surroundings anywhere I go. Wherever on the street I turn a veneer of faux always serves as a backdrop. Whetstones of glass hover above the ground in mass fragments of crystal. Enormous tree trunks of steel are imposed upon the skyline while its roots sink into the rock hard ground like fangs. I exist in this place impossibly small. Impossible to notice.

At night, bright and sickly colored lights seep and pour their radiation onto the streets. A dazzling, refined artificiality; every reflection in the glass and the stone and the concrete an impossible shade. Then, the horseless carriages awaken, howling and roaring in the night, their eyes piercing through the black air. Howling of sins and of curses and of disease and of their own afflictions. These carriages and their riders are afraid of what lurks in the shadows, for they are left vulnerable if apart from one another. That's why they always come out in packs. At night the city is at its most restless. Thickets and brambles of people close in and condense all around me, isolating me. I become completely submerged, growing lonelier and lonelier the more time I spend trapped in that shroud of bodies and souls. I, too, find my color slipping down the drain-but I don't feel its effects too badly. There wasn't much left to take.

Every morning now I wake up in a miserable haze. In my spare time I sit on the edge of my bed and float above my body for sometimes hours on end. I can't feel my skin, make out the contents of my bloodstream, sense the creases in my brain. I know they exist, I know that they're there, but I can't feel them. I fail to feel anything in this body. I also fail in recognizing myself. Whenever I look into the mirror, I am unable to recall a single feature. The moment I look away the face that was present slips from my mind, entirely forgettable. I splash sharp, cold water in my face and look down at that ever-leaking faucet.

Drip dry drip dry drip dry

I look up at the mirror again, trying to figure out the color of my eyes. Parse together the exact shade and hue. When I'm finished, it dawns on me that brown is not the right color.

Drip, dry, drip, dry, drip, dry

In the mirror, I try to familiarize myself with the bones in my cheeks, learn the curves in my eyebrows, memorize the shape and bent of my nose.

Drip. dry. drip. dry. drip. dry.

My eyes dart up again in desperation. Maybe the colors and curls and formations in my hair will stick to my mind. There's some strands of grey in there also. Remember.

Drip... dry... drip... dry... drip... dry...

I am once again unfamiliar with the creature that stares back at me.

I tell myself that if I can't, maybe someone else will recognize it someday.

Every day leaks and bleeds into the next. I get up to shovel coal and bring coal to blast furnaces. I spend the money I have leftover from rent on food because I don't know what else to get. I come back to the apartment and I shower and then go to sleep. I get up to shovel coal and bring coal to blast furnaces. I spend the money I have leftover from rent on food because I don't know what else to get. I come back to the apartment and I shower and then go to sleep. I get up to shovel coal and bring coal to blast furnaces. I spend the money I have leftover from rent on food because I don't know what else to get. I come back to the apartment and I shower and then go to sleep. I get up to shovel coal and bring coal to blast furnaces. I spend the money I have leftover from rent on food because I don't know what else to get. I come back to the apartment and I shower and then go to sleep. I get up to shovel coal and bring coal to blast furnaces. I spend the money I have leftover from rent on food because I don't know what else to get. I come back to the apartment and I shower and then go to sleep. I get up to shovel coal and bring coal to blast furnaces. I spend the money I have leftover from rent on food because I don't know what else to get. I come back to the apartment and I shower and then go to sleep. I get up to shovel coal and bring coal to blast furnaces. I spend the money I have leftover from rent on food because I don't know what else to get. I come back to the apartment and I shower and then go to sleep. Igetuptoshovelcoalandbringcoaltoblastfurnaces.IspendthemoneyIhaveleftc Igetuptoshovelcoalandbringcoaltoblastfurnaces.IspendthemoneyIhaveleftc Igetuptoshovelcoalandbringcoaltoblastfurnaces.IspendthemoneyIhaveleftc Don'twakeupdon'twakeupdon'twakeupdon'twakeupdon'

My benevolent landlord is never here. I can count on one hand the number of times we've interacted. How long has it been since I first moved in? He's always out on the town doing god knows what. I hear him come home late into the night sometimes while I'm lying awake in bed, trying to keep the bad, bad thoughts at bay. By the time I wake up in the morning he's gone again. I suppose all this isolation in a windowless room ended up being a blessing, I can't stand being around him any more than I have to. The times I did engage with him were all extremely distasteful. Our conversations consisted of nothing more than passive-aggressive jabs and bickering. Discussions akin to an old married couple with nothing better to do. My landlord and I, whenever joined together, are devoid of all substance. I can't get up on my own two feet because he takes all my money. I never have enough saved up since it all goes towards rent, but I can't leave or else I'll have nowhere to go. Ending up stuck on the twisted, knotty bones of the city streets, fighting for scraps. My landlord has carefully devised this perfect, endlessly looping prison. I pray one of these days to find the means to flee from his clutches.

Other than him, it's just me, myself and I. A battle of psychological warfare comprised of my own made up demons. Struggling for self-acceptance and reasons to keep this up. Searching within my situation for the means to be content. Stumbling towards the looking glass to face just what it is I'm made of. No way for me to properly handle these parts. No way of understanding why it is I'm like this. I never willingly chose to be this way. I know my crooked mindframe needs adjusting, but my own hands can't seem to tilt it back into place. I freeze to death before I can reach the top of that mountain. Fall from the sky before I can cross the tightrope. An insurmountable task. I have to work ten times as hard just to get to the same starting line as everyone else. I have a few ideas as to why.

One thing consistent throughout my life is that I have always been afraid of kindness. I don't believe I'm capable of receiving it. Upon being given such an acknowledgement my first instinct is to fight against it, searching for the truth I know is secretly buried under that goodwill or compliment. I don't have the guts to be gentle, it seems. Because of this fear I have barred myself from the one true human condition, love. Worst of all is love. Thinking about it now, it confuses me. Any ordinary person has an understanding of love that I've always lacked. What does it look like? How do you know whenever a relationship is based on love? I can't identify any of its features. The words used to describe it are far too simplistic. Simply put, I don't know what love is like. I don't know what its true nature is.

In all honesty I am unsure if I have ever felt love in my entire life. Maybe if I did have the ability, I'd be with everyone again. If only I could feel the love given to me and be able to give that love back to others, I'd fulfill the requirements needed to become a human being. But I can't.

All I can do is try and cope with the dissimilarity.

Another day going to work to do the same repetitive, meaningless tasks. Another day stuck in this apartment. Whatever people call this, having a job, being responsible, serving as a productive member of society, I can't stand it. I have no interest in it. Why is this the standard for going about the world? After going through these motions and being in the city for enough time, I am convinced that the ways in which we live are wholly antithetical to the actual wants and needs of humans. I am certain that we got the concept of living entirely incorrect. Not just as a result of industrialization, its roots go all the way back to the beginning of our inception. Since the dawn of civilization we arrived at the wrong conclusions and ever since then have stuck with them. This is not human nature, I'm sure of it. What we consider human nature is nothing more than the systems we place ourselves under. These ways and means don't interest me. It's all awfully drab and depressing. Where on this planet lies some true excitement?

My landlord told me not to look into that cabinet in the living room, but curiosity has already won. Something of value must lie inside it. After all, what's in there so important and precious to you that makes it worth hiding? Today, like any other day, is the perfect time to look. Today, like all days, he isn't home. His abundance of keys, used for various miscellaneous purposes, are once again missing from the kitchen counter. My existence lies at a standstill. A choice presents itself to me. I'm very eager to find out what's behind those maple double doors.

I stepped into the living room, making sure to take my sweet old time. I want to let this thing build, marinate, rise in anticipation. A reveal with no buildup is merely a morsel of ember, to become a fire the thing must be thoroughly stoked.

Slowly, I reach for the handles and gently pull. The doors softly squeak as they're pulled ajar. Just a little while longer. A little more anticipation. Then, in one massive heave I rip them fully open and peer inside. I turn pale instantaneously.

What reveals itself to me in that cabinet is a horrible, twisted, sickening sight. Before me sat a terror completely eldritch, almost Lovecraftian, in its presentation. A sight I thought I had been set free from.

Sitting on the topmost shelf is a glass box lined with medals. Medals that I am far too familiar with. Medals that celebrate death. Medals which are the antithesis to life. I curled up in a fetal position, my hands shaking uncontrollably. Of course I'd been forced to live with one of them. I should've known something was off about him the moment we'd met. He's an old friend of that stupid lanky officer, of course he was made into one as well. How many more of them must I endure, must I be associated with? My circumstances here aren't the greatest, but I thought at the very least it would allow me to leave that awful existence behind. I was wrong. No matter what sort of thing I do, war still haunts me. I have been permanently branded with the mark of a soldier. It's the only part of me people will ever manage to see. I live here with my landlord. I belong to the war machine by association.

He will get no more of my money. I don't care what consequences may follow.

I wake up and go to work then come back here. More time passes on and ever onward. My soul is merely a tick of a shade away from matching the hideous jade green of my walls. I've grown tired of all these hollow promises. All this self-aggrandizing disillusion. My mind made a mountain out of you, dear hope. But now I see that your house has completely crumbled. You had abandoned it quite some time ago. You were gone long before I arrived that fateful day. And as I watch your crumbled house it begins to shrink, condense, compact into a structure scarcely larger than a moles hill. That was your true form all along wasn't it? What you've been trying to tell me. "I warned you, desire comes with inherent suffering." You plucked that piece of advice straight from Guatama himself. Well, I raise you this question: If the path to enlightenment always results in giving up your earthly attachments, then what does it mean for someone like me who never had those attachments to begin with? I'll achieve enlightenment and become free from what? Turning one's back on the earth wouldn't do me much good. I have nothing to turn back on. Each perspective from every direction shows me the same, anthill sized, deteriorated home. There is nothing I can present to be sacrificed. I have nothing at my disposal to give you. I only possess one thing. A thing which I hold against my will. My only definitive tether, the only constant, is an emptiness that can never be filled. A sadness that will linger until the day I rot. One impossible to describe. One that does not stem from any external force.

These thoughts were interrupted as my door came into contact with a rapping knuckle. Before I even sat up, I had a rough idea of how this scenario was about to play out. I stood up and took one last relaxing breath before making my march towards that entryway. Swinging the rectangle wide, there stood my landlord waiting, arms crossed, firmly locked in the center of the doorframe.

"How come I have a rent payment that's missing?" his grim, unfriendly expression jutting out at me, foreshadowing some sort of impending doom.

"I don't have your rent." I said matter of factly.

"Now that's a problem. You knew when it was this month that you had to pay. But I didn't say anything. I figured I could trust you. I even gave you a whole extra week of leeway to let you pay it off. I thought, 'I'm sure they'll remember. They know what they're obligations are.' But I guess I was mistaken. Tell me, what's the issue? How am I supposed to trust in you living here if you can't meet your responsibilities? If I'm not careful, next thing I know you'll have torn this place apart." as he waited his foot, like a pendulum, went tap tap tap upon the floor.

"Well I–"

I began my search for an excuse, any sort of excuse, that might help to diffuse the situation. To assist in attenuating his cruelty. But my mind kept drawing formless inkblots that I couldn't recognize. I have to say something and say it soon. Why must I be so spineless?

Then his eyes squinted as he lifted a finger to point "What's that?"

I quickly looked back to where that finger was pointing to. On the nightstand next to the bed sat an envelope.

I turned to face him slowly. My eyes met his, they widened as he put two and two together.

In one swift movement, I snatched up the envelope, shoved the landlord out of my doorway, and ran. But I did not run for the exit, no, there was still something I'd been meaning to do.

I grabbed the fire extinguisher from off the kitchen wall and made my way to the cabinet. I threw its doors open with so much force that they almost came off their hinges. I pulled out the glass box with all its medals inside and shattered it, producing the sweetest note as it burst. That's when my dear landlord finally made it to the scene.

"What the hell are you doing?!" he cried. I detected a hint of fear in his exclamation. This certainly was one of the last things he expected to happen. I looked up at him in a crazed frenzy, raising the extinguisher so that it could be brought down upon those precious medals of his.

His fear was replaced with an all consuming fury.

"I'll kill you!!!" he barreled into me, the extinguisher slipped from my hands. He threw the first punch.

We twist and dance and warp our bodies down to the bone. Caught in a bloody and broken brawl like the unholy animals we are. That we were born to be. Nothing but our bare essentials. Our primal states. The cardinal way of being that military life has molded us into, reduced us into. Two titans who have lived for all of eternity, fighting for the earth and for hell and for heaven to see who reigns supreme, toying with cosmic forces in the process. Shaking the universe with each and every blow. A fight that becomes a matter of legend. A tale passed down through generations. That will be remembered for all time. If only a fight over some medals mattered that much.

I stand with bruises smeared across my face and my arms and my body, heaving and sweltering from the excursion. Blood pours like a chalice from my nose. My knuckles are all swollen. The landlord sits against the wall, arms loose and hanging draped along the floor, groaning like a dying buffalo. He appears to be in worse shape than I. He's trying to find the air for words, but is unable to. After several minutes of gasping he spoke.

"What the fuck is wrong with you?" he managed to let out. A series of violent coughs followed. His head began to shake uncontrollably as he murmured to himself. He flashed me a perverse grin as he finished.

"I shouldn't have let him convince me to take you in. I never should have let you stay here. All I owed him was a favor, you understand?" again he coughed.

Then he chuckled. Doing so entirely for his own amusement. "No wonder he dropped you off here and left. You're nothing but a nuisance wherever you go."

"To think you did all this just for some medals. A pathetic pile of trinkets." I quickly interjected. Beaming my eyes directly into his skull.

"Those 'trinkets' are worth far more to me than you are. Probably more than you will ever understand."

It took every fiber of my being not to unleash hell on this wicked, broken man. There were so many things I wanted to say. So many things I wanted to do just then, but I held back. I bit my tongue until it bled. Until the blood washed from my mouth all the bile and disease that dwelled on the roof and at the corners and in the back of my throat. With that my fate was sealed. I understood I couldn't stay here any longer. I need to be long gone by the time my landlord tries to hunt me down.

Hurrying, with all the speed I could muster, I gathered up all of the things I had brought and the rent payment I had saved. The last thing remaining was my badge of honor. I paused for a moment. I should bring that too. If I'm lucky I can pawn it off for a generous amount of money.

I went back into the living room and stood over my landlord who wasn't my landlord any longer.

"See what all these medals have gotten you?"

He didn't respond, just persisted in avoiding eye contact.

I left him there for good and took off. Dusk was beginning to settle in.

2.

Time has passed once again, and the rain still pours. The fire can't be felt at the moment, but I still see a faint glow traveling off in the distance whenever I look over my shoulder.

The city has been all sorts of unkind to me. Luckily enough, I found a nice spot under a bridge that looks out onto a river. This river is muddied and green with all the kinds of scum and rot you could think of. The steel beams of the bridge breach the water's skin and reach deep into its insides. I bought a reasonably sized tent to put in this spot, and it didn't even cost me that much. In spite of this, I ran out of money fairly quickly all the same. I still haven't found someone to sell my badge to. That is the key. In the meantime, I've resorted to looting and pillaging of all sorts and shapes. From time to time a fellow looter will join me in assisted deception. Whether it be at a convenience store or a supermarket or a gas station, both parties look out for each other. Helping to steal as much as we can without getting caught. Interactions are brief but always beneficial for the both of us, and every time it happens I manage to bring back to my tent something or another to get me through the day. That is the limit of my interaction with the outside world. Anything more than that proves to be too much. It's better this way, I've discovered. If someone were to approach me, what would I do? What should I say? If I ask somebody for any help of any kind it is unbeknownst to me how they will respond. The last thing I'd want is for someone to be angry or distasteful of me because I encroached on their life. That terrifies me more than any soldier or officer or battle ever could. I find people to be inconceivable, all of them strangers. My spirit has always been weary, and now it has become warped in distrust and skepticism. On the rare occasion that I do interact with another person, I find myself rewinding that moment over and over in my head, assessing my performance. How I did facing off against them and what

I could've done better. Promising myself to make those improvements next time, though it never does improve the next time.

Once I had properly situated myself under the bridge, one of the first things I'd purchased was an ice pack for all the bruises. There was also the gauze for my profusely bleeding nose. I recall that it did take a while for those to heal, but they as with everything else passed eventually. At the moment those wounds are but a distant memory. There are matters far more pressing that I need to attend to. For one the list of places I could steal from grows thinner each and every passing day. I may have to start begging soon. To grovel at the feet of countless passersby. Only accustomed to the familiar sight of splitting concrete. The tent has worked well enough for the time I've spent under this bridge, but I can tell my body is being slowly and meticulously worn down by the elements. I'm certain that the upcoming winter is going to kill me.

I know that I should search for help in order to survive, that it's the most rational solution under these circumstances, but something keeps on holding me back. A concern that far outweighs the tribulations of homelessness. I worry that even if society were to sympathize with my plight, that wouldn't truly fix me. If I were to live safely among others I still would not be cured. The rain would still fall. I'd still have cracks in the core of my being-and if you were to look inside, therein lies somewhere a fundamental fact. What has led me to this point speaks volumes about what I am. My incompatibility with those around me is crippling. I find myself asking questions that I already know the answers to. Projecting my voice, I call out to nothingness, expecting a response where there is none to be found.

I am evil because I can't fit in. My contortions have failed in giving me the proper shape. No matter what sort of bends I make they always come up short. All this time I've somehow managed to keep up my walls and my mazes and my illusions. That is how I appear. A puzzle piece that fits the whole well enough, but upon second glance you notice that the colors are mismatched. Its forms are all wrong. The edges are irregularly warped. To think I could fit into that mold without any struggle was a fool's errand. No wonder there was no one in my unit or nobody at the base or no letters or no one to pick me up. All my dispositions are incorrect.

And yet, after all this time, I still yearn for something. I don't know what it is, but I know now that it is something this world cannot give me.

I have come up with the theory that either this world is sick or I am its sickness. Maybe, somewhere out in the infinite expanse of the universe, there's a different version of the human race that I belonged to. One that didn't leave me stranded on an island in an endless ocean from the moment I was born. My presence on this planet is just an accident. I was sent here by mistake. My UFO unintentionally crash landed, creating one of the many craters on this planet that humans are so inquisitive about. I didn't anticipate my arrival here, but I emerged nonetheless from my ship, ready to learn the ways of this species. I never quite got it. I never did stick the landing.

I want to be normal, not whatever this is.

Throughout my time on this earth I've heard many people talk at length of the importance of being special. How in order to succeed in life you need to stand out from the crowd. That your uniqueness is what makes you great. Looking back I wonder, did those people even know the definition? Did they themselves ever experience it? The most tragic thing of all is to have uniqueness. The only thing being special has granted me is a one way ticket to alienation. A ticket which dropped off at a stop in the middle of nowhere long ago, and to this day I am still lost. Fumbling my way around in the dark. No directions for getting back to where I came from.

From time to time, I sit and watch people. I watch how they walk. Listen to how they talk. Notice the subtleties in each and every expression. See the ways in which their bodies bend as they laugh.

Study how those same bodies shrink when they cry or are full of fear. Then releasing that tension once they find a familiar face. There are so many things a person could be feeling at any given time. Most wonderful of all is the pure magic of a human being who is filled to the brim with happiness. Happiness so great that as they walk it swashes around like an unsteady cup, ready to spill onto the first thing they come across. Bringing a tectonic impact to all the strangers both in and out of their lives.

Some of these tendencies I recognize to be familiar, although it dawns on me now that I've only learned how to apply the pessimistic ones. I seemingly lack the full spectrum of complexity and intrigue that the rest of these inhabitants do. I'm left in awe. In spite of all my misgivings, I think that people are amazing, I really do. If only I could be one of them.

They hate me, they all hate me.

This mound of earth beneath my feet has broken off from the planet. I float farther and farther away with each passing moment. Where I now drift is the vapid void residing inside my mind. Swallowed and trapped by it whole. A ridiculous blankness that does nothing but inhibit me. Inhibits my success within the society around me and prevents me from achieving any role. These thoughts and confessions with which I toil have no place among the human race, yet still I find myself ceaselessly bound to them.

I have this persistent tendency to intellectualize my way into isolation. Apply "sound" reasoning as to why it's better being alone. Perhaps I just enjoy reveling in all of this melancholy. Creating a deranged romanticism and fetishization for an unhappiness that I have chosen to fashion into a twisted, mangled shield. This unhappiness must be purged, but each time I try I risk losing a part of myself. Is the only method for a cure to force cheerfulness and lie? To not be honest with others and with myself? What is my true self? I'm hesitant to give that question any answer. All I know is that if I am to be my true self, I will always be lonely.

Whereto, does the psyche fly? There are places and skies it has traveled that I could never comprehend. I can't leap.

I found a place.

It must be a basement of some kind or another. It goes much deeper into the earth than usual. Much more likely that it's a bunker. I found it on the outskirts of town in an abandoned building whose features are far too worn to tell of their past. I happened upon it by chance, completely blindsided by this sudden stroke of luck. It's hidden underground well away from the city's watch. Never for me to be bothered. Whatever it is, it hasn't been lived in for decades. Rather one of those places where only the shadows lie.

A jug with cobwebs frothing at the mouth sits in one corner, so dusty and worn down that none of its color can be made out. In another is a shelf that holds only a small set of wheels meant for a chair that isn't here anymore. These wheels stay motionless in the second-most bottom ledge. I see no reason to move them.

Now there isn't any bedding of any kind down here, but I was able to move my tent and all of my sleeping supplies into this basement. It's perfect. I couldn't ask for better.

The Edison bulb that dangles from the ceiling is so very dim, and some nights when I turn on the switch it's a gamble whether or not it will flicker to life. When it's on, I can see the shadows dancing every now and then. Sculpting their shapes and silhouettes into the light. Although I'm not sure if I see them when I'm awake or when I'm dreaming, or if awake is just like I'm dreaming.

Where I now reside is quite certainly on the outskirts.

I never was able to pawn off my medal. Not one transactional relationship was made with it. That's no good. I wonder, why the lack of interest? Maybe it has no material value, contrary to what I believed.

Fortunately for me, this new place I've found comes along with new places all around to steal from. This could very well be my new strategy from here on out. Migrate from different areas of the city into new ones where any recognition is implausible. This place is quite large and ostensibly endless, like jaws that forever are closing in. I could take my tent and my bedding with me. I'd last a long time this way, leeching at the underbelly of this concrete jungle. Defiantly resisting death like a cockroach. A pest. Navigating all the places to best scavenge off of. If this must be the role I take on, then so be it. I am on the brink of starvation, and there is no more time left for me to use up. I'm on the brink of one too many things to count, in fact. I'll strike when the city comes the most alive, and pass to and fro like the wind.

I am not.

It's nowhere near as dense as I thought. That's strange, it's always packed like sardines in this place. As I look around I notice the typical rows upon rows of people filling the streets have grown unusually thin. Unusually barren. Already my plans are being foiled, the cover I rely on unpredictably taken from me.

No matter, I can still be in and out of multiple places before I'm noticed. The silver lining is that I now have more room to scuttle around. I brought my pillowcase in order to store as much as humanly possible. Or rather, what's possible enough for a cockroach.

Already, I've taken from three separate places. My case has been filled with a rather adequate amount of things, but I still need more. The more I can get now, the longer I can go without needing to come back. One more place. One more place should do it.

It's a convenience store that is rather small. Much smaller than I'd have liked it to be. In fact, the average school district classroom is larger. To make matters worse there are only a few others in the store. A lot less than I anticipated, but I'll make do.

Quickly and silently, I move items from the shelves and into my bag with one fluid motion, grabbing mostly nonperishables. Any items I pick up that can perish go straight to my stomach. A few berries here, a grape there, several bites from an apple or a carrot, really the first things I managed to come across. No matter how my gut wails I am careful not to leave any trace or evidence. This has gone well so far. I've made my way about the entire store and still no signs of conflict. However, the most challenging part of this task is yet to come. Getting out. I must leave without getting caught and the register stands right in the periphery of the doorway. Peeking around from behind the furthest aisle, I watch the person who mans this register. Just as I'd have liked, they appear disaffected and uninterested by their surroundings. Searching deeper than that, I unearth a resounding discontentment which resides in the face, buried under layers of skin and bags in the eyes. Pushed as inward as it possibly can be in order to get through the day. Now is my chance.

The cashier turns slightly to help a waiting customer, and as they turn I make a moderate bolt for the door. Keeping my steps and my pace even, never once changing velocity. The double doors sway gently open. I turn, head down, into the street. I made it. Now all that's left to do is crawl back into my hole.

Then, just as my mind had made shape to this thought, a voice with the force of a bullet bored into the back of my head.

"Hey!"

I don't know why, but that voice was enough to stop me dead in my tracks. Despite every instinct and piece of cognition telling me to run, I didn't. Couldn't. Instead I slowly let my head swivel round to face the cashier and their tired, sunken eyes. Teeth clenched, I could tell he was already over this. I noticed his left eye beginning to twitch.

What I didn't notice were several figures on the side of the street smoking and sighing. About to sink into a brief moment of relaxation, all wearing this cashiers' same uniform. Their relaxation, unfortunately enough for me, was interrupted by this shout. These figures then gave a collective grumble. Several cigarette butts flicked to the curb as they began to rise. The cashier nodded, giving them a knowing sort of look.

Before I knew it I was on the ground, each blow growing duller and duller until senselessness crept in. A senselessness which continued on for quite a while. Then the figures all together stopped and abruptly headed back into the store. Already their break was over, and I was left pressed against a stone wall. My items spilt and strewn like fabric across the concrete. I was too weak to move, the mechanisms in my body grinding to a halt. The city continued moving onwards for a long time. I still couldn't

Then another voice made its way towards me, this one far more subdued and merciful than the last.

"Are you ok?

I raised my head, mouth hanging wide open as I gasped for air. What greeted my vision was a little girl wearing a smooth, satin sundress. Her hair reached just past her shoulder blades. On her feet were weathered sneakers that I could tell had seen many adventures. A dirt that was pure and clean, far removed from the dirt I had come to know.

I couldn't bring myself to answer her, let alone admit what I had done. Rather, what I attempted to do. She looked down, awkwardly shifting around on the balls of her feet. After a few moments she brought her hand out from behind her back. From this hand she presented to me a mangled chocolate bar that was beginning to melt. Half of it had already broken off. Hand and arm extended to me, she gently smiled, giggling softly. I took the piece of chocolate and gave it my first bite. It tasted like a pile of dirt, the sweetest thing I'd ever felt upon my tongue. It annihilated me, this chocolate bar and this little girl and that giggle. It was too much. Never before had I felt the impact of something to such a staggering degree. I felt as if I had been throttled to death by her warmth. I choked back on my tears, nearly unable to face her.

She looked around at the aftermath of my struggle, then back at me.

"You're gonna need that stuff. Mommy's saying there's not much of it left."

"What does that mean?" I asked.

She shook her head briefly "I don't know. All mommy keeps talking about is how we're going to travel. She never tells me where. She always just says we're traveling somewhere far, far away from here."

"Why is that?" I asked.

"She doesn't tell me, but I think it's because everybody else is traveling too." she said. Tilting her head slightly, she began examining me.

"Are you gonna be traveling?"

I let out a faint smirk "No, I don't think so. I never made any plans. I'm not really sure where to go in the first place. I don't know where I'd end up."

The girl thought for a moment, index finger resting on her chin. Then her eyes lit up and sparkled.

"You could come with us. Mommy's been having a hard time since Daddy's been gone. She's always trying to do everything. Do you want to travel with us?"

This offer brought me pause. I never would have expected this to be a choice. Mulling over the options at hand, it was apparent to me this was the most logical path to take. No longer having to fight for scraps or fumble around in the dark. I could get support from this little girl and her mother. Could this be the start of the new life I was searching for all along? I looked back at her delicately.

Then it dawned on me.

She was happy. There was nothing in her constitution that suggested otherwise. My constitution, in sharp contrast, was the embodiment of misery itself. There was no outcome in which I joined that wouldn't inflict damage upon the both of them. In no time at all, I would spread upon their lives like a canker, eroding at all the humanity they had. It would ultimately be cruel to subject the girl and her mother to such a grave consequence, especially after being gifted with this lovely offer. Where was her mother anyway? I should send her back. Even without being a part of their journey, already I have driven a wedge between them.

Kindness is not meant for the weak or for cowards. Therefore kindness is not meant for me.

I politely smiled "That's alright. I don't need to travel. You and your mom will do just fine together. In fact you should probably go back to her. I'm sure she's getting worried by now."

She shrugged "Ok, if you say so." and went on her way. That was that.

As I watched her scuffle off down the road her mother suddenly turned the corner. She quickly gathered the little girl up into her arms with a worried but relieved expression on her face. She started asking the girl things, until eventually the girl twisted around to point at me. The mother began eyeing me with suspicion. Then I blinked and they were gone.

I'm not sure how much time passed after that, but I eventually found the strength to get up and head back to my bunker. The city's streets are nearly empty in spite of the setting sun, its lights far dimmer and far less in number. What would usually be the moment in which swathes of people appear never came. Even the wind is failing to sing its usual song. I sense an infection spreading. When I let it into my head, I cannot recall. The items I lost are now nothing but an insignificant memory. The feet I walk with have grown heavy, burning with each passing step. I can feel the creature following me with its eyes, putting me under constant scrutiny. A whisper passes through me, describing in great detail ghastly, harrowing thoughts. Wounds which have torn themselves open again. Profuse bleeding that never does stop. I can't discern whose voice carries these whispers, but with each and every instant they grow louder, louder, louder.

I retain nothing. Possess nothing. There is nothing left for me to do. I have no one for comfort or to comfort. No one to hold and to be held by. No one even simply within my vicinity. I run my hands along the lengths of both my arms, trying to supply myself with something, anything, to fill the need for contact-but it's no use. Already there is a frigid shell beginning to form itself in a ring around the edges of my heart. I can feel it starting to whittle me down to the bone. I can feel it slowly killing me.

I dwell in my bunker once more. I've almost figured it out, the voice that whispers in my ear.

The shadows, the shadows dancing on my walls; dancing in malicious enjoyment. A sort of ghoulish joy. They have finally revealed themselves.

It is the world whispering to me. Refuting my argument. Dismantling the idea that the way in which it operates is antithetical to human beings. It tells me that predicament was never the issue. It is impossible for that to be the issue because there is always movement. The world still turns and people still endlessly rise despite all of the bad. In the face of adversity this world still is able to maintain itself. Everything on the planet can operate to some degree, able to do so in order to get by. Everything except for me, the fundamental error. The shadows continue to dance, their movements growing ever more erratic.

It is I who am antithetical to this world. It is I who am the sickness. The distance between myself and other people is far too great. An impossible gap I can't ever bridge. I need to die. If the world is to continue I need to die. That is the final truth.

To think I could be able to get a read on anybody. To think I could understand and properly assess the depths of the human condition. In the end, what was it I set out to do? Draw back the curtain and reveal the hypocrisy of the human race? Offer up truthful insight as to what human beings really are? What simplistic nonsense. Such lack of nuance. The only thing I've learned in all my years is that I will depart from this earth as clueless as when I entered into it. What right do I have, attempting to draw these lines of designation? Everyone experiences hurt, plenty of pain and anguish goes around and comes around. If it's possible for me to feel this way then there are already millions of others having done so before me. Why should others care about my afflictions? Afflictions as pertinent as a speck of dust in the eyes of the universe. We all are stuck with towering levels of stumbling blocks which threaten to buckle and collapse at the slightest mishap. What makes me, of all people, so special? I have made the most monumental of errors. I have inadvertently become a narcissist, indulging myself in a forlorn hubris. This is the greatest of all my sins. I need to atone. I must be punished.

The Edison bulb begins to flicker. The four grey walls of my bunker bask in a pale, sickly orange. As I draw closer in on one, the shadows scurry off, traipsing into the blackness. I look deep into the features of that wall. What appears to me is a sudden inclination. I then give back to the world my response.

Against the stone, my head begins pounding.
And pounding
And

                                                      Pounding
And

                                                      Pounding
And

                                                      Pounding
And

                                                      Pounding
And

                                                      Pounding
And

                                                      Pounding
And

                                                      Pounding
And

Pounding

And

I am awoken by a deep rumble within my chest, the breadth of which I have never felt before. I place one hand over my heart to see if the rumble results from an incessant knocking. It doesn't.

I place the other hand on the floor. I can feel the rumble spreading across it. It's spreading across everything in the bunker. The shelf shakes as the wheels bounce against it, eventually rattling off onto the floor. Then, a loud clash, something akin to thunder, burrows a muffled bellow into my ears. This is not thunder. It is something all too invariable and precise to be considered thunder.

They found me, they must have found me. They know I murdered the lieutenant. This is their retribution. All my constant running away proved to be ultimately futile. I have finally been caught, their mechanisms of death now preparing to close in on me. As fast as I can scramble and as much as my balance will allow, I reach for the bunkers door handle.

Darting up the steps, I think about all the strangers I have come to know. I wonder for a moment where they all are now. Maybe serving the war machine, or preparing for another hard day's work, or traveling, or going mad. Thinking about these things spurns a reasonable thought which comes to cross my mind. They have all continued on in some way. There is the basis that everything about them and more will pass. Just like my fears and my sins and my melancholy. The world tells me that even it too, will come to an end. That it will cease as the sun implodes. Crumble to dust as time always and forever gouges away.

This reassurance from the world is enough to move me to tears. No other being has offered forth such closure and contentment to me. If it is I who must perish, then let it be so. Nothing much will matter to me anyhow. I could have done this or changed that. Gone about things differently. Accomplished some goal that would vaguely resemble meaning something. But no matter what I will be forgotten. Thank god, I will be forgotten. I finally understand, I'm strong now.

Thank you for the hopelessness.

I arrive aboveground at the scene of my abandoned block. Off in the distance, though I am unsure how off, a mushroom cloud begins to form; a gentle breeze traveling from its outermost ring. From in and around my periphery, smaller but faster explosions sprinkle themselves onto the ground and throughout the roads and into the buildings. Almost directly above me a fighter jet soars. From its underbelly drops a bomb. It will land on me in no time at all.

It explodes on impact. Bursting forth in a swath of red and orange and dirt and shrapnel. The bomb tears me to shreds. Rips my body asunder.

And at last.

At long, long last.

I am free.

<u>Epilogue:</u>

I can hardly believe the abysmal destruction that makes up this place. Any trace of any location has been wiped off the face of the earth. A constant stench of death follows me wherever I walk, no life to be found anywhere. Atrocious doesn't even begin to cover it. The only thing that has entered my field of vision in the past several hours is rubble. Witnessing just the aftermath alone of such immense suffering is enough to make my knees buckle-but worst of all is the fact that all this never accomplished anything. It was all for nought.

The human race repulses me, and it has for quite some time now. It's all just one massive concoction of cognitive dissonance. From birth, we are taught critical ideas and distinctions on how to live, what's right from wrong, methods and guides on going about the world. Yet history, and this current war, has made it rather obvious how willing we are to stray from these teachings. Abandoning all morals when push truly comes to shove. People say and preach things, stand upon their soapboxes at every possible opportunity, and never once take a stand when it really matters. Always backing away once it becomes too inconvenient or uncomfortable to handle. But I suppose I've no room to talk. I'm just a pretender. When the time came I didn't have the guts to fight. All I did was refuse to join their war until my stubbornness made them give way. As a result I've been assigned here to this city in order to sort through all the debris. Salvage, collect, preserve what I can. Report any potential findings. Most importantly, findings we can use as an advantage against our faceless enemies. What I do is shameful, really. Instead of making any real, authentic difference; I quiver in fear and retreat to something easier, something that will allow the cutting of corners. But I think that even if I did try, all I'd be doing is getting in the way.

I regret not taking another path. Any other path would have been better than this. I should've made my escape when I had the chance. I can only dream of what the future may have held if I had. Much to my own disappointment, I was too afraid to ever try. I probably deserve this, the consequences of my utter inaction. Oh well, it's best not to dwell on it. I just hope that I have the strength to act when it matters. I wouldn't be able to handle the guilt if I resorted to cowardice again.

I'm angered by a lot of things, but right at this moment, the thing that annoys me the most is my current coworker. All he does is babble on and on about the things going on in his life, things I couldn't care less about. Even worse is when he talks about his past. Every time I can tell when he's about to. He does this thing where his eyes travel up towards the top of his head, all the while sighing and beaming softly. Then, he recounts his oh so fascinating "glory days," as he calls them. The whole ordeal is nauseatingly pompous. You'd think the least he could do was be interesting when telling his stories, but I can't help but grow bored the moment I hear the phrase "bygone era" slip from his mouth. Ever since we got assigned to this job together his stories have fallen on deaf ears.

"Hey, why so glum all of a sudden?"

I jolted up from the trance I was in and looked back, "Oh, nothing. Sorry. I'm still very tired from the long road trip we took to get here."

"Hey don't worry, I totally get it. Going back and forth between all these places to clean up somebody else's mess sure is a drag huh?" he grinned.

"That's definitely one thing we can agree on." I replied.

He cackled "You sure are funny, you know that?" he was still grinning, but for the first time I detected in his voice a note of disdain.

Then he brought both hands down on both knees, "Welp." He opened the truck door, "Better get started while the sun is still high."

"Right." I nearly whispered.

I don't really know how much time had passed, but the sun was starting to get low. All this searching and the only things we've managed to find are a few rifles, someone's flask, and a uniform so shredded it is impossible to recognize. All that was thrown in the back of the truck.

There's all the charred bodies of course, but those can't be used in any practical way.

Surveying the whole scene once again, I notice the small dot that is my coworker way off in the distance. He is standing on a hill of bricks doing god knows what. The one thing I'm certain he's not doing is continuing our search. This frustrates me to no end. Is he purposely making this job take longer?

But after a second thought, I realized the job that was tasked to us is inconsequential to begin with. I have my doubts that any of the things we bring back or have brought back the war machine actually has use for. We aren't useful to them in any capacity. The main reason we're here is so we have something to do. Because if we don't, that gives us time to think. And nothing is more dangerous than that.

Then I notice the small dot in the distance get suddenly shorter. Is he squatting? No, is he on his knees? Don't tell me he's praying or doing something similarly ridiculous. After a few minutes of watching the dot shuffle around, he abruptly grew still. The sound of brick shifting ceased. A deeply unsettling silence was in the air. A true silence. One that lacks the sound of running water and the chirping of birds and even the wind. Shuddering, I quickly turned back to whatever I was doing. What was I doing? Something, anything. As long as I can fill my head with noise.

Quickly I grew bored again. There isn't anything worthwhile in all these piles of heap. It's all useless, useless, useless. If we do manage to find something "valuable" in all the wreckage, what benefit will it serve to anyone? Its only purpose would be to aid in furthering our own destruction. The only way we know how to win is by killing each other, regardless of how much we kill ourselves in the process. All our genius and ingenuity is invested in that. Never once have we invented true understanding, sincerity, or peace. In all of the thousands of years this human race has lived, you'd think there'd have been a breakthrough by now. It's funny when you think about it, how inept we are despite being the most advanced species on the planet. I guess being alive is the only unsolvable problem we have.

"Hey, look what I found!"

I see my coworker speed walk back over to the truck, shuffling here and there in order to get over loose stone. I ended up leaning next to it after a while. He's waving something in his hand, but his fist is clenched too tight for me to make it out. As he gets closer, I notice that whatever's in his hand is glinting and reflecting from the light of the sun's golden, falling rays. It is a piece of bronze.

"Check this out."

Opening up his palm, he revealed in it a badge of honor.

He whistled "Wow, what a find! This is the last thing I expected to be among all this other crap." Even for him, he was acting unusually cheerful.

"I bet this is worth a whole lot. Say, why don't we find someone to sell it to? I bet we could make a fortune! That'd be so much better than giving it back. A real waste, in my opinion."

I gazed deeply into the inner workings of this medal. I wonder who it belonged to? And how did they end up in this place? I don't know why, but I felt a deep sadness echo in me then.

"Well." I said, "Whoever it belonged to, they must've sacrificed a hell of a lot to earn it. There are few and far between people with such great levels of courage. I can only imagine the strength, the sheer force of will, that granted them such a badge. If only I could be brave like them..."

I couldn't finish the thought. The guilt and shame I was carrying became too much. Teardrops soaked into my face and into the bricks beneath my feet. My co-worker stood next to me awkwardly. Neither of us said or did anything for a while.

Then surprisingly my coworker spoke up, "Don't beat yourself up about it. It's like you said, most people don't have that sort of strength. What matters are those little, insignificant moments. Ones where having courage doesn't mean such a grand gesture."

I wiped away the tears and watched the grey clouds floating above me. "All I want, all I've ever really wanted, is to make a difference for just one person's life."

He placed a hand on my shoulder and spoke to me gently, "Don't worry, I'm sure you will. And who knows, maybe you've already done so. Just know that I understand. Forget about selling this badge. Let's make sure we honor them, whoever this soldier was."

Our eyes met, and we smiled at each other for the very first time.

About the Author

Samuel M. is a life form that dwells on the planet earth. It's entirely a mystery how he managed to end up here, but he manages. He's interested in all sorts of things, but above all is his love for the peculiar. He can't help but become curious whenever something has a peculiar edge to it. Whether it be an object or a living thing or a work of art, he is always delighted to revel in oddities. For oddities are what make the world go round.

www.ingramcontent.com/pod-product-compliance
Lightning Source LLC
Chambersburg PA
CBHW071325130726
47996CB00002B/631